MASQUE -RADE

A DI Alexander novel

STUART BONNINGTON

Title: Masquerade
Author: Stuart Bonnington
ISBN: 978-1-7640500-1-2
©2025 Stuart Bonnington

This is Stuart Bonnington's third novel following
the career of Detective Inspector Linda Alexander,
and his fifth book in total.
His previous publications are:
What's It All About
Murders Galore
Three Very Different Women
87 Not Out

A catalogue record for this
book is available from the
National Library of Australia

DEDICATION

To Jay for her support and patience

CONTENTS

Chapter 1

The Body in Fitzroy Gardens
Event 1: Murder

AAn early morning call to 000 certainly caused excitement about activities in a circus. A hysterical female voice said a clown was lying dead beside the pond in Fitzroy Gardens, near the Conservatory, in East Melbourne CBD. The caller stated the clown had been beheaded.

Coincidentally, Detective Inspector Linda Alexander was just arriving at work at Police HQ and as the location was almost on her doorstep, she quickly decided to attend. On arrival she found a local uniformed constable had it ribboned off even though it was only 7am. The pathologist arrived within minutes and everything was made secure. It needed to be, as a few early-morning walkers, animal minders, and simply curious people were gathering.

On the surface the event was already macabre, with a decapitated body, and it became more so, and bizarre, when Linda saw a note attached to the torso which read, 'No more clowns; no more leaks!'

The body was clad in extravagant circus clown clothing of bright colours including excessively sized boots and gloves. The gloves had the fingers burnt off and each finger was damaged. Arms and legs showed signs of injury. A large round black cap covered half of the severed head exposing dyed black hair. The face was heavily made up, emphasising a huge red mouth painted in bright red lipstick, the eyes outlined in black, a big bulbous red nose and green pixie ears. It was quite a sight.

The constable now had extra help to control the gathering crowd and Linda was able to ask the attending pathologist some questions. The initial responses included that death occurred about eight hours before, victim not killed on-site, blunt instrument trauma to parts of the body, violent injuries to arms and legs, plus burning to fingers—re removal of finger prints? Decapitation and body left to bleed out beside pond. Male, approximately 1.7m in height and not overweight. The rest would be speculation because of the makeup. Clothing had no brands, head appeared to still have own teeth; that may be useful. Full report to come tomorrow after autopsy. Linda could anticipate an interesting investigation.

Perhaps rather illogically, but because of recent bad press, Linda speculated to DSS Beth Jenkins and other members of the urgently gathered special police team whether or not some consideration should be given to a connection with a new small group of masked right-wing fanatics recently given to parading in Bourke Street who left their protests with Nazi salutes. They had been known to park their cars in Lansdowne Street alongside the gardens. The chants of 'destroy paedo freaks' and 'men can never be lesbians' helped incite hatred and prejudice. The masked fanatics were known to seek publicity and stir opinions where they could. But what was the meaning of the note?

Chapter 2

DI Linda Pretorius Alexander
The day before Event 1

Detective Inspector Linda Alexander is enjoying a rare weekend at home. Her home is a stylish apartment of two bedrooms, two bathrooms, in a high-rise block on the corner of Spring Street and Flinders Lane in East Melbourne, opposite Treasury Gardens and in the so-called 'Paris end' of Melbourne CBD. Living on level 18, she has owned this apartment for three years. A quiet haven in the middle of a busy city. She is accompanied sometimes by her new partner of almost two years, Jacques (Jack) Classen. Jack is a senior officer in ASIO so while both are in the security services, being in different organisations means the relationship is unlikely to spark any conflicts of interest in their work life. His parents were immigrants from Holland and he was born in Australia.

This Saturday, they ambled around hand in hand in the Treasury and Fitzroy Gardens and almost wandered into a noisy protest on the steps of Parliament House in Spring Street, by Bourke Street. A big turnout including a large group of uniformed police and four on horses, apparently there to separate right-wing activists from counter-protesters demonstrating against anti-trans activists. Noisy but not overly aggressive, but provocative by making the Neo-Nazi salute—commonly known to older people known as the 'Heil Hitler' salute. There have been serious demands to have white supremacist organisations banned. In many people's minds they are in the same criminal class as bikies. Linda and Jack moved quietly around the different groups as they enjoyed their anonymity. Apart from walking around the beautiful gardens, they often enjoyed strolling to the local Princess Theatre in Spring Street, or the Regent Theatre in Collins Street, for shows.

Linda had never questioned Jack about whether he was a 'spook' but was well aware he would have signed the Official Secrets Act and no doubt was used to using encrypted correspondence. She was not sure if he was involved in counter-intelligence or counter-terrorist operations.

That morning they were simply enjoying one another's company as they strolled down Collins Street to find a quiet coffee shop. There they had a very light lunch, as they wanted to shout themselves a special upmarket supper this evening at Ronnie Di Stasio's 'Citta' (City) Restaurant to celebrate their being together for two years. Right next door to where they lived. Not far to walk home! Today was a lovely Saturday afternoon in the sunshine in March as summer was declining and winter knocking at the door.

The dinner appointment was for 7pm so Linda and Jack tidied themselves up in casual but smart clothing and went next door. Being totally off duty they enjoyed the suggested dry vermouth while they considered their meal choices and the beauty of the restaurant. Ronnie Di Stasio, often referred to as Rinaldo, was well known as a patron of the arts. His establishment was of modern design featuring brushed concrete and marble. Linda had only a smattering of Afrikaans among her foreign languages, due to her South African heritage, and Jack admitted to none. Certainly, no Italian. The beautiful Citta menu contained words like Stuzzichini, Le Paste Caccelone, Spinaci, Formaggio, and Di Stasio Affogato

Liqueur. However, the explanations from staff were quick to come and most helpful.

Aterwards, feeling full, warm, and contented, they went straight home to their warm nest. Without rushing they removed their clothes with big smiles on their faces and started the touching and cuddling precursor to their trusting, mutually enjoyable sequences of sexual intercourse. The murmurs of pleasure as fingers entered those sensitive areas and heightened expectations. Silly little ditties sung or rhymed together as they gradually became more entwined. Without need for more preliminaries Jack was inside her and they could both feel the heat and huge pleasure as a relief and pleasure of the highest order. Wonderfully compatible and with time to enjoy each other, they gained warm, tender pleasure from one another, each empowered to experiment in agreed ways.

Next morning, Linda was aware of Jack cuddled up alongside her back, half naked, half-asleep, wrapped around one another, as he softly awakened her with a "Hello" and gently kissed her fully awake. Their unit was quiet and secure. Protected by a double entrance at street level, a 24-hour concierge service and personalised lift access, there was no way unexpected visitors could arrive. It was more about security and excluding people from any aggressive activities permeating the units. Even their private cars were protected. For them security was paramount. They wanted no one unwanted to be able to intrude into their relaxed home. The biggest intrusion was the daily newspaper dropped outside their unit's door. Of course, telephone calls, emails, messages re food deliveries, and pizza could still get through!

On the Sunday morning, with the pair both feeling relaxed and happy, another round of glorious lovemaking began. Nakedness of body, mind and soul could be achieved in their 'fortress paradise'. Neither one could remember such prosaic matters as whose job it was to make tea, coffee or eggs for breakfast.

Linda and Jack were appreciative of their rather rare moments together, when they discussed not much more than the exhilarating physical sex and banal day-to-day subjects but so far no in-depth 'deep and meaningfuls' about inner personal feelings or plans for the future. Linda spent much time studying to complete her MBA. Jack, as a senior ASIO agent, had his own private status and was privy to much secret service information. However, seldom was his life put on the edge of the precipice. Not to say that he was never in serious danger though.

Linda had worked her way into a senior Detective Inspector (DI) role at the Head Office of Police in Victoria. Her position was secure and she had a trusted team of associates around her headed by the slightly younger Detective Senior Sergeant (DSS) Beth Jenkins, who had asked to be promoted from a previous plainclothes position at the peri-urban Woodend Station to widen her role into 'serious' policing. The trust and friendship between the two went back many years. Linda was in charge of many Police Unit sub-divisions including money laundering and international contracting. She reported directly to another long-term associate, Superintendent Ron Brunton. Currently the small team was busy but slightly bored by the routine of checking on an internal police subject titled 'The Greater Utilisation of Resources and Capital Expenditure.'

No doubt jealousy pervaded parts of the huge regime that was 'Head Office'. Like all big organisations there were constant unofficial internal discussions about retirements, promotions, rivalries and opportunities. Jockeying for positions was constant and an eye and an ear was always open. At this point, it was no secret that Superintendent Brunton was nearing the end of his very successful and popular tenure.

Linda often thought of what a protected childhood and adolescence she had enjoyed. It seemed incredible that she had been in the police for so long, that she had never had a 'wild and woolly' stage in her life, or been involved in erotica or into drugs. she had always been all very correct and staid! Linda reserved discussions about those type of things for meetings with her long-term friend and police associate DSS Beth Jenkins. Nothing was off the table for their 'girlie' chats. Sometimes they'd meet in this mode every week, other times a gap of more than a month would elapse. Good friends.

Chapter 3

A Small Circus
Event 2: Fire

A small circus performing at the Steam Engine Park Reserve, just off Station Road in New Gisborne in Central Victoria, hardly seemed important, but the uniformed police at Gisborne Police Station were advised by the CFA that they thought there was something strange about a tent fire there, and reported it further up the line. Superintendent Brunton, knowing DSS Beth Jenkins lived in nearby Woodend, suggested to DI Alexander that Beth might like to 'look in' on the location. Circuses are transient and can move on quickly. Everyone was pleased for Beth to carry out an inspection. Small, neat and blond, in plain clothes Beth was unlikely to engender any hostility.

Beth arrived and was surprised by the modern look of all the support vehicles and the youthfulness of the circus staff and associates. The fire, which destroyed one of the several generators on site, looked professionally done, as was some other damage to the enclosures for horses and goats. Happily the animals were too well looked after and trained to want to make an exit.

Beth was well received by all, and asked the usual questions about enemies, dismissals, staff, any old family grievances, any outstanding finances etc. She also discreetly asked more personal questions but she was met with hesitation over the question of any LGBTQ associations by some of the staff, who looked away before answering 'certainly not'. The circus seemed to be fully integrated with the small food providers and side shows where prizes could be won, mainly by children throwing balls at hoops.

Beth was impressed enough to take one of her children to a matinee performance on the following Saturday. No free tickets were involved. The marketing must have been good as parking was crowded. There was plenty of bright music, and the ticket office (part of one of the caravans) was efficient with both cash and cards. Popcorn, soft drinks, and hot and cold food were sold from another van and other vehicles were parked in such a way as to provide toilets and to block access to the circus animals. All very neatly and professionally set up. It seemed the whole entourage totalled around twenty-five persons.

The big tent program was simple and basic. Dynamic acrobatic aerialists and trapeze artists clad in beautiful garments, a well-organised Ring Master who was involved himself in some of the acts, and a couple of comedian clowns with a broken-down car that fired water at them and the audience. Lots of whip cracking and a modified act of apparently cutting an assistant in half. The major activities were clearly controlled and carried out by the Ring Master. It was not quite a one-man band, but almost. Beth wondered to herself whether the little circus was family-inherited or purchased. It was very family friendly. There was no extreme behaviour, costuming, music or noise. No smutty jokes or innuendo. Three goats and three horses provided light relief and a quality variation act.

Beth observed that all the kids loved it, no-one was apparently smoking and exits were well organised. As she was leaving, she saw a car parked by the entrance that had a little sign on the door with the name in small print of another circus. On enquiry, the name turned out to be that of the largest circus in Australia, mainly owned and run by close traditional family members. Was a competitor checking out this little circus in New Gisborne?

Beth's report back to Linda was 'No obvious criminality. No finger pointing by anyone. Presentation and operation of all parts and associates of the circus seemed to be within the law. Clinically clean and family friendly. Enquiries indicate no problems about insurance (or lack of it), and no one injured or out of pocket'. Case closed.

However Beth then went on to speculate about possible damage to routines and dates to be fulfilled, if a major part of a circus was damaged.

Chapter 4

The Biggest Circus in Town: Coopers
Event 1: Murder

There were no reports of missing people, and police contact with all known circuses indicated there was no missing clown or any other worker. Establishing the identity of the body was proving difficult. The pathology report was quite simple. Death by violence at a separate location. Stomach contents showed the remains of a pizza and beer meal, a blood sample showed a small amount of cocaine. Some application of torture had been made to the arms and legs of the body, but not to the face or other parts of the severed head. Closer inspection indicated some form of injection had been made between the first and second toes on one foot. The gruesome discovery of stitched-up eyes under the clown makeup was taken to be an added 'message'.

The area by the Fitzroy Gardens Conservatory was searched in detail, and that was widened across to the nearest roads to search for any delivery vehicle marks. The police opinion was that at least two persons and a trolley of some description must have been used. The quality of the makeup and the obvious effort to disguise the victim in 'no brand' clothing meant an effort had been made to delay identification for some reason.

Linda quickly asked to have Beth Jenkins added to the team to inspect the location of the biggest circus in town. This turned out to be a site near Broadmeadows in northern Melbourne. Because of the experience Beth had previously accumulated it was decided DI Alexander would accompany her on a visit.

This was a seriously big circus. On arrival it was clear there was a hierarchy to be observed. It took several questions and some patience before they were taken to the caravan of the senior couple of the family. Police qualifications and identity had to be proved before John and Cora Cooper made the two police officers carefully welcome in their sumptuous mobile home. They were middle-aged or older and had a sense of style and assurance about them. The home was surrounded by other caravans and mobile accommodation with very interested spectators, and Linda and Beth could sense an element of mild hostility to their presence in 'the inner circle'.

After pleasantries were exchanged, John Cooper asked the obvious question, "How can we be of help?" Linda took a colour photo of the deceased and asked them to comment on the likely origin of such a clown. Could they tell anything from the colours, style of makeup, hat, boots, etc. Almost in unison was the answer: "Certainly not one of ours! In fact, never!"

Linda explained that this was a brutal murder and the victim and perpetrators completely unknown. She was keen to establish that John and Cora Cooper were the owners and operators on a daily basis of the full activities of the circus, as they had quite distressing information and more photos to show them. Confidentiality was requested and quickly given in the affirmative.

The Coopers response to the further details was equally firm, and even appalled. The clothes and makeup of the so-called clown was not of their 'style' and no one was missing. Over a friendly cup of strong black coffee, a quick inspection of the facilities was offered. The designated guide was one of the Coopers' adult children who worked in the circus, the oldest son, Marko. He was around 30 years old and clearly second in charge.

As a quiet aside, Beth almost immediately commented to Linda on the less than friendly attitude shown by Marko and the contrast to that offered by his parents John and Cora, and the sheer size and sophistication of this very modern circus. The tents and associated mobile buildings were modern and functional. Physically Marko was big and strong and handsome in a mid-European way. A thin black moustache and sideburns added to his exotic look. He offered that he was Australian born. He told them he was aware of the clown murder.

Marko was happy to explain his place in the history of the circus. He emphasised that he was not the Ring Master and neither was his father these days. He explained operations at length and showed the officers photos of some of the more spectacular acts. No animal acts these days, he explained. Clowns, trapeze and acrobatic dynamic aerialists, colourful lighting, bright and bold music, combined with death-defying highwire acts, motor bikes, swordswallowing, small people and magic were all standard fare. There were clowns in various guises and inflatable clothes jumping on and off cars, bikes and horses. None of the old 'bearded ladies' or 'freaks', and no tolerance of alcohol or drugs naturally as it was too dangerous in the high-risk acts.

It was all pretty much as Linda had expected but she was impressed by the quality and cleanliness of all the equipment.

There was less exuberance from Marko when Beth raised questions about OHS rules and regulations, and hiring and firing of the more casual, less skilled staff. He was almost dismissive in stating that most employees came from within the family and were well taken care of and rewarded. As expected, when asked if anyone was missing, or had potential enemies, the answer was an emphatic "No."

Also as expected, when asked about his whereabouts on the night of the small circus fire in New Gisborne he was vague, but confirmed he was on-site with other personnel of their family circus. Marko finally took them back to the luxurious caravan that was the home and office of his parents, and said he would answer other questions if needed. The same statement and a formal goodbye were received from his father John.

The casual enquiries made to date indicated that the highest profile of any member of the family belonged to the staff member known as 'Jack the Rabbit', who had free-ranging responsibilities with the circus. As part of the senior management team who plotted future venues, his job was to search for suitable sites and negotiate the terms and conditions for the circus to be domiciled there, for how long, and at what price. Because they were often quite delicate negotiations, Jack was envied by some of the other family members as he was always ahead of the circus, well dressed and with a nice car as he carried bright promotional material to spread around. A natural entrepreneur with style, he hid his homosexual tendencies. Jack had a substantial budget, mainly in cash, to use to swing negotiations if deemed appropriate. It was rumoured that alcohol, drugs and women were also used on occasion. Jealous ex-employees had over the years alleged many irregularities by Jack. He had a big responsibility to lock in the forward schedule, however always with approval of John the boss.

Like many family members, Jack had the natural abilities of an actor. Some had graduated to other roles within the circus. Some members were benign and friendly with cheerful eyes, some seemed menacing, and as in many groups, psychopathic types were always hard to pick.

Linda ordered a full investigation of both Marko and 'Jack the Rabbit', including childhoods, education and any history of violence or drug use.

Chapter 5

Police Work: Clown ID

In the car going back to the Police HQ, Linda stressed the need to identify the victim. Exactly who is he? Can DNA or any other method help to establish a name? Australian or other nationality? Beth volunteered to do the hard yards of contacting all the other active Australian circuses to see if anyone was missing or had known violence with any associates—other circuses like Wirths, Silvers, Circus Royale, Eronis, and even those who were still playing on the extremities; Stardust and Lennon Bros too, supposedly descendants of the famous Perry family. She would try to establish if there were any old enmities or rivalries. It was well known that in older circuses the family had to be a "jack of all trades" and turn their hand to anything that was broken.

Linda expressed to Beth her satisfaction about the discussion and integrity of information from John Cooper but felt far from happy about Marko. She considered him to be arrogant and 'shifty'. She commented, "Let's do a really full check on Marko. Any drug connections?" Linda then offered the opinion that local police members often had unofficial contact with some casual workforces, and just maybe some with contacts in a circus could help?

Back in the office, Linda spoke to her boss, Superintendent Brunton, simply to update 'No progress yet, and no pressure being applied from any source.' She added that she may yet need to add to the size of her investigating team. Linda and Beth made an appointment with the pathologist to discuss the situation and to view the body, expecting to see the cleaned cadaver with all makeup removed and the body parts in normal position.

The pathologist offered the opinion that the cutting of the neck was precise and the cause of the clown's demise. The person under the disguise had been fit, clean and tidy. The clothing was all 'no-brand' including underwear, the shoes and socks were not Australian, but also not from Asia, and the black hair was not dyed. He was of mid-European appearance and clean shaven. His teeth were well maintained and he wore a quality watch. There was nothing in his muscle development that would indicate a specific trade or profession.

The makeup had been difficult to remove and in the pathologist's opinion expertly applied. The big nose, excessive mouth emphasis, the pixie ears, all made the face initially unidentifiable. Stripped bare, quite a good-looking person had emerged. The white gloves and yellow wig were extensively covered with dried blood.

Linda and Beth almost simultaneously asked the same questions; Time of death, weapons used, locality of death? Then "Performer in a circus—Australian, or obvious other?"

The response was "More precise details in a few hours."

Linda reflected to Beth, "Sometimes it's hard not to do; but don't compare your life to others. You have no idea what their journey is all about."

Chapter 6

Marko Cooper: Suspect

Enquiries began in every direction. Linda and Beth telephoned friends and contacts within various Victoria Police divisions, the Australian Federal Police (AFP) and contacts in ASIO. Posing much the same question, "Do you know of or have you ever experienced a criminal or victim of crime who has a record of impersonating a circus clown? Linda also sent inquires further afield to New Zealand and the USA, and specifically to the New York Police Department. Speculation in Linda's first special team meeting was that it must be a payback or warning to some group or person as there were no claims of responsibility for the killing, no obvious drug, sex, or cash connections involved and no known gang retaliation.

More concentration was given to the type of personnel involved in circuses. Were they mainly actors or more like a series of individual cults based on family? Was there a jungle of 'their own' and, as suggested by one constable, the Ring Master may be the one to investigate first, as they were traditionally the 'Lord and Master' and had been known in the past to be cruel to staff and animals alike.

Linda concentrated her enquiries on the eldest son Marko and his siblings. With the help of a seconded constable, she established that Marko had attended boarding school in Auckland from the age of 13. The school was a rugged environment with only 100 boarding boys along with 750 day boys. The boarders had established a reputation as a small cult-like regime that looked after 'its own.' On initial introduction to the system, the young Marko had had no appreciation of how it would form him. Luckily, he was physically robust, good academically and smart enough to mature and easily fit in. Initial teasing along the obvious lines of Marko, Darko, sparko, farto, For Maggio, etc, produced tears in his eyes in term one, but such teasing of Darko diminished soon after he confronted a slightly older boy with a well-aimed punch to the solar plexus. Any ideas of further bullying were put away after he sneaked into his locker a large and sharp-looking knife from the circus which he declared had injured a patron in an act. In spite of his swarthy looks at this bastion of whiteness, Marko gradually became well liked and respected by masters and fellow boys. Academically, he advanced through the curriculum with ease and had the potential to pursue many careers.

The boarding facility was basic to say the best thing about it. The buildings were double-storied and had long, old-fashioned hallways up the middle with dormitories upstairs, and the administration, sick bay, dining facilities, small gymnasium, locker room, showers, toilets, and washing facilities all downstairs. The buildings were old and wooden and in a previous life the school had been a convent or hospital. Rumour was that it may have been a mental hospital.

Marko was a good team boy and fitted in well with boarding school routine. By the time he was 16 he was an integral part of school and boarding functions. He was up early helping with 'new kids' welfare, assisting in meal arrangements, washing, locker honesty, and the necessary controls to allow quiet study times. He was involved in informal supervision and control of dormitories, helping prefects and masters. He was destined to be a prefect.

Linda was told routines were simple in that the boys each morning had to run around the block at 6.30am, shower (lukewarm at best), then get into school uniform for a sit-down porridge and fruit type breakfast, and finally with teeth cleaned they were off to school by 8.30am. They were expected to be tidy in fully conforming uniform. Clean shoes, socks, trousers, cap and jersey in winter. That was a big ask as often gear was lost, so then the loser could be in trouble. The prefects had a range of powers to add to their authority. They could issue a thing called a 'fatigue' that was registered in the 'Fatigue Book.' Too many fatigues could transpose to punishments of many varieties; e.g. working in the garden, cleaning a prefect's shoes or, in a worst-case offence or accumulation of fatigues, a whack on the behind administered with a roman sandal of the school uniform type, by a prefect. A bruising was expected to be seen next morning in the showers. Punishment handed out by a prefect eliminated the record in the book.

Marko's family was of Roma, or 'gypsy', origin from Romania, and full of history going back over many generations, both in Australia and overseas. John Cooper, his father, had a full memory of all the pain, the racial ugliness, and all the accidents/tragedies and cruel humour he and his forebears had been exposed to. The family had developed their own strength through these incidents and sad reflections. John could well remember being called unsophisticated and not 'smart'. His brother, 'Big Paulie', was a giant who wore a black singlet and was teased as being 'thick'. He was a gentle giant with big warm eyes and strength enough to hold all the gymnasts aloft. He could be a very deliberate clown, falling over his big feet just to get a laugh. John often wondered how anyone today could do a real apprenticeship for such a career.

John and Cora Cooper were determined to have Marko involved in the business, the main reason being that John had some serious health issues.

Chapter 7

The Cooper Circus

Upon finishing high school, Marko was absorbed back into the family circus in Australia. He had forgotten, or maybe had not even been aware of, the hierarchical manner in which his father ran the business. The intensity of all living together was not that different from the boarding school regime. For the first time in his life, Marko observed blue veins prominent on his father's nose and face. He also noted some slurring of speech which his mother also carefully noted. It was probably due to alcohol and ageing, and being a smoker could be contributing to some dementia, Marko thought.

John's management style was 'old world' and very family-oriented. The wealth of the circus assets was well hidden. Management meetings were reasonably open and younger members were encouraged to attend and listen, and to honour confidentiality. There was an overall informal style but the real authority was very clear. Sometimes a small reference to police and overseas connections was dropped into conversation. Always the importance of the paying customers was stressed, and using modern methods of finance and abiding by government rules and regulations.

In contrast to the open nature of the management meetings, John and his Ring Master stressed the need for secrecy in the use of IT and taxation matters. Matters such as money laundering, illicit affairs, were spoken of in lowered voices and with caution: Not circus business! The Cooper Family Trust was referred to, but it was considered much too early to inform Marko about it in detail. That would change practically and over time by a form of osmosis— the slow exposure to him of facts and figures, history, slights and memories of rivalries and hatreds going back generations. Terms such as 'fruit of the poison tree' and some family being spoken of as rotten to the core were heard. Young family members were encouraged to record and remember history particularly where they had been put down in public. The hatreds were used as family anchors as well as binders.

John and Cora Cooper had been brought up on the old truths and myths and had in many ways used them to strengthen their own leadership. With signs of oncoming dementia, time was now of the essence. The circus 'family' included fringe entertainers: ventriloquists, puppets, scary dolls, and fairy floss, hot dog and pizza vendors. No drugs were allowed. The family admitted no connections with any relations from the USA. Many of the artists were of darker complexion with long hair and moustaches. There were lots of children and many dogs and other pets.

A surprising amount of property was owned by family members and staff including some places that looked like junkyards. For a short period of time, Marko owned a flashy V8 Commodore and motor bikes, as did a few other members, all of whom mixed together over a beer with a variety of diverse 'friends'. Linda compiled a full report.

Chapter 8

Second Murder: Coincidence?
Event 3: O'Brien's Circus

Almost simultaneously another murder was reported in mid-city Melbourne. The victim was a partly disguised man in slightly made-up appearance and wearing colourful baggy trousers. His body was found early in the evening suffering from stab wounds to face and abdomen. He was taken to a local hospital where he later died. The forensic pathologist reported that the injuries had been incurred before midnight and the heart had been pierced by a very sharp instrument.

The case arrived on Linda's desk for any obvious connection to other crimes to be useful for identification. DNA and all personal clothing, wallet, teeth and shoes quickly identified the most likely identity. Family was called in to confirm it was Rusty Williams, known to the police as an active member of the small country O'Brien's Circus, and of dubious ethical standards, currently active on the fringes of Bendigo in Central Victoria. Testing revealed that Rusty Williams had consumed large quantities of alcohol and other drugs. Senior Sergeant Beth Jenkins, with the help of Senior Constable Gerry Flowers, was allocated the responsibility by Linda of investigating Williams, with a focus on any potential connection to the Melbourne CBD 'Headless Clown' victim and rivalries or any associations.

O'Brien's small country circus was a real 'jungle' of its own. It was O'Brien family owned and operated, mostly with underprivileged associates and employees, and run like a secret society. Most payments, where possible, were made in cash, but remuneration included free food, free accommodation, the use of a battered old car and moral support in any situation arising. Most members of the team were undereducated and had inferiority issues, even though they were very skilful in their own areas. Tattoos were plentiful and the use of alcohol and drugs was extensive. There was a known association with some members of a major motorcycle gang from Adelaide.

This circus team prided themselves on their hierarchy, their family history, their own policing and the skills they had within their own unique framework. They were their own musicians, electricians, plumbers, electronics engineers, builders of the stands and seating, and responsible for their own safety, security and animal welfare. Everything else was incidental.

It seemed to Beth that records and details of both casual and permanent employees of O'Brien's were a little on the light side. SC Flowers held her breath when Beth suggested to the Ring Master and owner Patrick O'Brien that the records were incomplete. He just smiled as if to say, "Go on, charge me!" He liked to say, "Our circus employment motto for casual work is, 'Come one, come all', and that is what we practise." However, he was willing to help with the possible identification of one of his 'family'. It soon became clear that the deceased Rusty Williams was no saint, and had probably been a drug dealer at some level, but certainly had no connection to the 'Headless Clown' found beside the pond in Melbourne. Rusty Williams had been easy to identify and was quickly eliminated from the suspects in the Clown crime. Further enquiries from Linda's special group were deemed not necessary. Linda was not sure about that, however, as Williams was known to be active in drug and alcohol trading and probably in association with a bikie gang, and thus by connection probably in money laundering, even human trafficking.

More and more it seemed that perhaps the first victim, who had been dubbed 'Bozo the Clown', was an illegal immigrant, without a proper visa, and maybe from the USA.

Rusty Williams had seemingly been a small bit player in a much bigger plot and he was unaware of the motive for his killing. It became apparent from local investigations that he had procured supplies from a middle man using burner phones and cash. Almost anonymous.

Chapter 9

Cousin Franko in Melbourne

Cora Cooper was a member of the Grasso family. She and her sister Lucia were second-generation Australians and their children. although cousins, were not close. They lived and worked in different arenas. Lucia married her husband Costa in Melbourne and their son Francisco was educated at Xavier College in Barkers Road, Kew.

Frank, as he chose to be known, sailed through secondary school with all the help possible from his aspirational parents. This meant daily, weekly, termly, and yearly special support in all school and sporting activities to ensure he graduated with the best possible qualifications for a commercial career. Mother and father had done everything possible to have Frank mix with the 'right type' of friends and families. He did very well at fulfilling the promise and developed an arrogance out of proportion to his achievements. At one stage during a rowing regatta amongst elite Melbourne colleges, he and some of his collegiates were caught and censured for openly urinating over the dividing walls where Melbourne girls were rowing. Sheer arrogance.

Despite several similarly small but insensitive actions, Frank was accepted into a form of apprenticeship with the large accounting firm PWC. He was able to live at home, subsidised in a lifestyle beyond most of his contemporaries. Frank had adopted a motto of 'Anything to get ahead.' He was good at clowning around, had an easy manner, and with his black hair and good looks, and plenty of money at a young age, he attracted a similar group of friends and companions. It helped his status to have a small MG sports car.

Little of the way of life of his circus cousin Marko and his family was known to Franko. He had heard his parents refer to the circus family as the 'academy of fools' but being remote relations emotionally, he had never visited the circus.

It was an absolute surprise that by a sheer fluke of circumstance the cousins met. They were introduced at a promotional fund-raising event at a luncheon on Lygon Street, in Carlton, Melbourne. It was an unusual event for either to be attending, but had been arranged by a local Lions Club to raise funds for the family of a Collingwood AFL club member. Franko's father had sent him along for connections, and Marko's mother had seen it advertised in the local newspaper in Brunswick. The fact that their mothers were sisters could easily have gone through to the keeper, but more by luck than good management it was Marko who recognised Franko by his surname, Randazzo.

It was a good opportunity to connect and chat together, as the long-lost cousins they were. They recalled some family get-togethers from a long time past. Frank was naturally gregarious and because of his easy lifestyle and confident manner, inclined to show off. Not long into the fairly one-sided interchange, he alluded to the fact that he could supply some recreational drugs at the 'right' price, as he was a legitimate purchaser and trader of stocks and shares and works of art. Marko was astounded, astonished that someone could be so brazen and open. The chat finished and they parted ways.

Back at home at the circus, he passed it all on in very lowkey fashion to his mother. She had no comment but later confessed to husband John she had been speechless, adding what a huge gulf existed between the families. Quite genuinely, John and Cora had never used drugs but were not naïve enough to think they were not in use amongst their own staff. Several members of staff and a few members of the family had been terminated as employees over the years. The luxury living conditions the Coopers offered were considered to be enough to protect and deter the 'team' from such activities. Tolerance had been extended over longer periods of time for younger members to indulge in noisy V8 motors, open exhausts, and some only-just roadworthy motor bikes. Who the younger brigade mixed with was not closely monitored.

The Cooper family were aware of having remote family connections in the US and an even more ancestral heritage as Roma, or gypsies.

Chapter 10

US Beginnings: Codona Family

Hatred over generations and the sins of parents go back a long way for many immigrants.

West New York, along the Hudson River, was settled around 1790 by Dutch immigrants around Bergen. It was known as part of Jersey City and was directly west of Manhattan Island. Lying on the Hudson River adjacent to Weehawken was an industrial community and a manufacturer of apparel silk and leather goods. It was a lawless area. Sometimes known as 'Havana on the Hudson' recognising a Cuban history, even today the single largest ethnic population group is Puerto Ricans. The diversity mix with the biggest numbers includes Italians, Irish, Russians and Germans. Added to the mix are large numbers of Africans, West Indians and Chinese, and many more minority groups. A real melting pot.

The early Codona family first arrived in America in the early 1900s and immediately began doing what they knew best. The family after many generations had grown to well over 100 members currently sharing the surname. The most senior member of the New Jersey family was known as 'Romy' and was revered by the family and feared by enemies. In the early 1900s, as the most senior member of the Codona clan, Romy was elderly and very powerful. Traditionally, they were Romanian Gypsies and known as traders and entertainers. They were renowned for fixing things and were sometimes called by the derogatory term of 'tinkers'. They were wonderful musicians and innovative dancers, who traditionally fiercely guarded their own independence. The Gypsies, or Roma people, were considered only to be short-term employees and that allowed them to maintain their high level of family loyalty.

Some worked in travelling circuses, some in amusement parks, some sold goods door to door, having been either purchased cheaply, or in some cases acquired as settlement for unpaid debts. They were traders. It did not take long for the Codona family to put down a firm basis in New Jersey and to become involved in the world of manufacturing, and in selling imported goods from Europe plus locally made products. Many forms of trade existed as did a form of simple money laundering, and when and where appropriate there were loans to 'friends' and family members. A type of mafia control existed in New York and the existence of another player quickly became known. Many forms of family protection grew up. Romy's eldest son, Patrin, took over after Romy died, and he was now the most senior member.

Patrin's two sons became an inbuilt family protection system as they matured. The oldest son was Credi, whose name had Italian origins meaning 'Just', and the younger brother was named Hanzi, a word within Romany history meaning 'God is Gracious'. Not much stock was ever attached to the meanings by the parents, Patrin and his wife Penelope.

When the boys were younger, the stories from their grandfather Romy had enthralled them. Grandad had clear memories of his own childhood in Romania with its intertwined stories and myths. They were colourful stories, with heroes and villains. Wars between neighbours, countries, towns, friends and enemies. They all seemed romantic and vibrant. The family made the relationship more real by arranging for Credi and Hanzi to visit their grandparents' other family in Romania on two separate occasions, even though they were still quite young. Some of the more fantastic people and events that had been circus legends filtered into their brains.

The Codona family in the US grew into a large group with diversified interests including illegal and legal activities, mainly around their home base in New Jersey. The very old saying 'A dictator needs no supporters; he just needs followers' was a true axiom in regard to the Codonas. The family had deep investments in commerce and active participation in circus life.

The time between the two world wars was vibrant and chaotic. Prohibition in the US provided wonderful opportunities for fortunes to be made by united and ruthless groups. This description applied aptly to Patrin (Pat) Codona. He was charismatic in his own way and loyal to his family group—cousins, uncles, and a wider range of relatives. He was athletic, attractive and charming. The most trusted member of the group was Pat's second cousin, also called Romy, who had children much the same age as those of Pat and Penny. The growth of activities was slow and confidential and well managed. Family activities were regular and happy. Financial strength was taken for granted and the family and children lived comfortably. The family lived and observed Catholic traditions.

Sons Credi and Hanzi had important responsibilities in the group. After finishing high school, they went into the family business. Hanzi was quicker on the uptake—had a real head for buying, selling, and making a profit. Credi, as the older brother, was much more solid in his attitude and personality, and liked detail. Credi worked closely with his father's cousin Romy, while Hanzi, with a personality more like his father's, was more the 'marketing man' and a charmer.

Following family traditions of improving their education, Hanzi and Credi were enrolled in night-school studies in commerce, banking and finance. They enjoyed their studies because Hanzi, in particular, had benefited from the holiday visits the brothers had as children to their grandparents in Europe. The brothers often chatted about how big the 'real world' was.

Hanzi and his cousin Romy's daughter Katarina became great friends, even though there was an age difference of three years. No one seemed to notice or care, until she was around fifteen years of age. Slowly over the years, Katarina stopped calling him Hanzi, and he stopped calling her Katarina. They began using the names of 'Hans' and 'Kathy' and became much friendlier to each other, not publicly or too obviously, but signs were witnessed often enough to arouse concern in the family. It was clear they were becoming ever closer, and it was deemed enough for a 'word' to be given by Pat about the importance of how things looked as well as how they actually were.

Katarina aka Kathy grew into a young woman playing an important role in the administrative affairs of the group. She was well liked by her peers but quite unworldly because of the isolation in which the whole family operated. Her experience with members of the opposite sex was nil and the family gypsy culture intended to keep her that way.

Almost to the day on her 16th birthday, she and Hanzi aka Hans, were walking in the twilight back from delivering some clothing to a local customer when Hans leant across and boldly kissed her full on the lips. With total and fully automatic reaction, she wrapped her arms around him and kissed him back with enthusiasm. They moved into a slightly more private space in a doorway and kissed some more. Breathing heavily, they looked around guiltily, hoping they had not been seen.

The small size of the family group meant that Hans and Kathy were more often occupying similar spaces and were able to exchange smiles and looks of warmth. It did not take long for them to begin clandestine meetings, be they ever so brief. The reality of what they were doing soon set in, and soon they realised their love for one another. The secrecy made their emotions so much more intense.

The physical consequences quickly developed, as did a plan to 'escape' their restraints. Hans in his own right had some savings and had many contacts within the shipping and transport arena. Kathy had little or nothing above a tiny amount saved from family gifts on birthdays and religious days. Hans began enquiring among his most trusted friends about possible pathways and costs to move to England. It did seem to be easier to travel in an anonymous way on a 'tramp' type vessel than would have been thought. Explorations on the subject went on for months as the danger of the relationship intensified. Kathy was now almost 17 and determined to be treated as an adult. In his saner moments Hans realised he was playing with fire but could not restrain himself. "I love you!" was now an often-exchanged utterance between the two.

Family members were aware of some aspects of the current situation and more than aware of the potential developments. Pat and Penny were not renowned for tolerance or forgiveness. Credi took it upon himself to have a word with his younger brother, giving him a mild warning that he had heard rumours about he and Kathy, and that if true, she may be sent away to Chicago to relatives for a year or two. All said in a moderate fashion and received by Hans with noncommittal thanks.

Things progressed at a frightening speed, as they do when people are so young. Hans' job put him in contact with all types of traders, both legitimate and rascals, and his enquiries had led to his being able to buy cabin accommodation from New York to England. He was soon in touch with a rogue captain of a small 'tramp' ship, a gruff old German who needed not much other than a fifty percent cash payment up front and recognition of the necessity of extreme secrecy because of the obvious risks involved. Hans assembled all that they would need and considerable cash and valuables.

A date and time late at night was set for Hans and Kathy to arrive dockside in full clothing and wigs disguise, in sync high tide. They arrived on schedule at midnight and began boarding but with Hans halfway up the plank, the captain ordered it withdrawn. At the same instant, other equally disguised family arrived dockside and grabbed Kathy and tore her away as she screamed, "I love you, Hans! I'll follow you soon!" The family members who had captured her muttered to themselves, "Bloody unlikely."

A miserable Hans had an uncomfortable trip to England, and he was informed that the fifty percent cash paid upfront would pay for his one-way trip, and the captain had nothing more to say to him. They dumped him unceremoniously, with all his belongings, on a remote beach in the UK. As a young man under 20 years of age, it did not look very promising for him.

Kathy was treated quite differently by the family. Not with much love but with a whole new set of strict parameters on her activities. These new rules were made even more stringent when she confessed to her mother that she thought she may be pregnant. The clan moved with surprising speed. All agreed, "We need to marry her off and keep the baby as one of our own, as most surely the child is a Codona."

Pat and Penny secretly agreed between themselves that once the dust had settled over the terrible event of son Hans 'absconding', they would make unending efforts to find him to seek revenge for his disloyalty and theft from them. In his wilder moments, Pat was heard to mutter, "I'll kill the bastard." No one was sure if he referring to his son or the ship's captain or others involved.

The solution Kathy's family came up with to the problem of her pregnancy was deemed a great cleverness by the family. It was to immediately select a new partner from within the Codona clan, marry the pair gypsy style, and then she could advise all that she was pregnant. The new baby when born would be described as two months' premature, and so accepted within the larger family. Terrible for Kathy but agreed by all the others involved as problem contained.

The anger that emanated from Hans' father Pat, however, was never contained, and he was heard to say often over many years, "Even though he was my son and stole my money, most of all he was family! Where was the loyalty! I can never forgive him. I expect generations to follow this up for repayment." That meant revenge, and to eliminate forever the remote possibility of Hans ever turning up to reclaim parentage of the child, now claimed by Kathy and her new husband and second cousin Alessandro Codona as their own together. The baby girl was named Maria.

Pat and Credi together vowed to never forgive, and put into practice their promise by putting a reward out for information on the whereabouts of Hans. They stipulated that identity must be beyond doubt, and the reward was to increase in size as the years went by. It was assumed that searches would be carried out in the UK, Europe or even Canada. The bounty on the head of the 'disgraced' Hans Codona dead or alive was set at US$100,000 plus an extra $10,000 for every year that went by without a result, to keep the hunt 'alive'.

The reward became known and infamous internationally because of the influence of the family involved. Hans was known among the circus world and Codona family as the 'Most Hunted Man'.

Chapter 11

Hanzi (aka Hans) Codona

Hans had an uncomfortable time on the UK beach and had no idea where he was. More by luck than good management, he found his way to a tiny village where he sat with hands on his head, until a friendly local took it upon himself to invite him into the pub and buy him a drink. Hans spun a story about being an American on holiday, and gave himself another name. As he had his money and stolen family valuables, he was able to get accommodation and clean himself up to look presentable. The English were very helpful.

It took some time but Hans managed to finally to arrive in London and procure a job on the wharves as a common labourer. He was a very quiet, conscientious worker. He had grown a substantial beard but after a while he realised that England was not a safe place to remain. A close friend in the US had let him know there was a bounty on his head. Always now on the lookout to 'disappear', he saved every penny he could, and constantly sought chances to grab another anonymous berth aboard a 'no questions asked' ship.

He spent most of his days looking nervously over his shoulder while he grew his beard longer and bushier, and acquired two small discreet tattoos on his arms of crown and anchor, to be like a sailor.

He focused on learning to speak like an English local. He had very dark eyes and a dark complexion, reflecting his Roma heritage, and in neat clean clothes he tried hard to be anonymous.

Quite quickly, Hans learned to use local colloquialisms and became more invisible and mobile. He really enjoyed the humour that existed amongst the seaside labourers, and was determined his future trail would not be followable. He created a plan to go in a very convoluted path, working casual day jobs mainly labouring (in any field), through Europe via Romania to Turkey, where he had been given 'business' connections. Because of his trips to Romania as a child he felt he would understand the language there. When he finally arrived in Turkey, initially just as a stop-off, he made substantial dollars as a bouncer in a whorehouse.

Hans made valuable criminal contacts in Turkey before heading to Africa where he hoped to join the French Foreign Legion and disappear from future detection. Hans' looks were changing and he had physically hardened up, as had his persona. He was also building up considerable cash wealth. He joined the French Foreign Legion (which was famous for asking no questions) and loved its requirement to use a completely fictitious name!

The French Foreign Legion (FFL) was established in 1831 as an elite group for men aged 17 to 40 years of age. With four divisions there was scope for all skills and nationalities. The Foreign Legion had a huge emphasis on fitness, fidelity and honouring the uniform and culture. Training and loyalty were paramount. Many recruits did not make the grade, but Hans loved it and excelled. He was soon identified as a soldier the officers could trust and to whom he gave unflinching loyalty. Small promotions were earned, which gave Hans a wider range of contacts for the future.

Hans stayed years in the FFL before deciding it was time to consider establishing a new permanent identity. He happily went along with every command given, but after one accident where he was injured in a brawl with another Legionnaire, he asked the surgeon to make his slightly prominent ears smaller. He then let his hair grow longer for more of a disguise. The FFL surgeon was an expert and was prepared to significantly aid altered appearances. With mirrors and diagrams, he explained that the eyes were crucial, the nose was easy but best to leave the lips alone. As time passed, the face would 'weather', and the nose would sharpen up to look solid and warm. The surgeon suggested that for a full disguise, Hans should invest in framed glasses with plain lenses, and told him how to acquire a new name.

French Legionnaires who survived the early examinations and tests clearly regarded themselves as members of an extraordinary mercenary corps. For Hans, it had been like a new, trustworthy family. It became part of him. There was also a dark side and big doses of reality associated with many of the FFL's activities. It toughened him up in many ways.

On leaving he made his way down through Tanzania, Zimbabwe, Namibia and finally to South Africa where, with the help of significant cash and the Second World War missing persons list, Hans became legally Jonathan Samuel Smithson, aka Jon. Many certificates and amounts of cash changed hands along the way. He was now a 'real' person again; this one suntanned, slender and physically fit, and very vicious if necessary.

Jon very deliberately set about embracing his new polished look, new name, new but very private family history, a fictional childhood education, and a cover for his smattering of newly acquired languages. No marriage or children in his history. To further cover his tracks and make any potential tracking down of him even more unlikely, he decided to move to Perth, Western Australia, and become an Australian citizen.

The series of new identities he had adopted had made him ever more careful, untrusting and unable to loosen up. He had developed a passive 'hostile' courage. For protection, on the surface he appeared to be quite mean and bitter. Jon also knew that a real escape was only possible within his ability to acquire enough wealth, be it local cash, US dollars or euros, or gold and diamonds, to allow him to be a 'king of the road'. He considered Africa in general to be a bad, corrupt place, but it offered a wonderful opportunity for him to accumulate serious quantities of illegal cash and other wealth forms, which enabled him to buy even more useful contacts.

He needed additional certification for the strict Australian entry, but once in Western Australia he discovered it was not known as the 'Wild West' for nothing. Jon decided to move on to Kalgoorlie which had a deserved reputation for the availability of big earnings with not too many questions asked if cash was produced. Jon stayed in Kalgoorlie for almost a year buying and selling, and cultivating contacts, before moving to Melbourne in Victoria.

Jon Smithson was a standard, ordinary name. Jon had worked hard to acquire what he was now said by the Australians to have—a 'pommy accent'—along with his new polished look. As soon as Jon became confident of local customs and lore, he made an appointment to meet a lawyer with a reputation for extreme discretion. This was a basic requirement never to be varied.

His instruction to the Melbourne lawyer was to employ what could best be described as a 'private eye' agent based in Chicago, for remoteness from New York, to simply act as a 'listening post' for activities, action or communications relevant to the bounty set on the life of Hanzi Codona by the New York family. The utmost confidentiality was demanded.

Chapter 12

Jonathan Samuel Smithson
(aka Hans Codona)

In Melbourne, Australia

The years in Australia were kind to Jon.

His office was now also his current home. It was on the 38th floor of a high-rise apartment building in Spring Street, East Melbourne, where he enjoyed privacy and security through the building's 24/7 concierge control. One of his companies had bought the apartment off the plan and he had an interior decorator furnish the whole apartment as part home/part office, and additional security had been added. The enormous lounge/living room had floor to ceiling windows with north and south-east views, over both the city and the Treasury and Fitzroy Gardens, and as far away as the Dandenong Ranges. Triple-glazing, slightly tinted, added to privacy and safety. Air conditioning, expensive tiles and appropriate carpeting added to his comfort levels. Hidden or discreet cupboards made it all modern, as did the chosen pastel colour scheme. Lighting could be changed from low to garish if needed. It was all a long way from average, and protected by hi-tech IT and security systems. The added security enabled a separate room to be very secure, and another part of the apartment to be separately entered and locked with its own dual key setup. Hans' early commercial training as a teenager in the USA

39

was not wasted and he had lost any obvious US accent. How had he become so successful? Firstly, he was tough and ruthless, and not known to Victorian Police. 'JS' as he was now known within his inner circle—such as it was—had become extremely wealthy by utilising a number of attributes; a quiet confidence, extreme patience, confidentiality, (in reality, no real friends) and he owed no favours. He had no family. He took further steps to register as an Australian citizen with dual citizenship which, with assistance from his international 'business associates', was not difficult to achieve.

Jon had the time and money to spend on his greater plan before moving on. Even by his own standards he could be hardnosed and vicious. He noted that the so-called drug lords who did get caught and jailed had the money to appeal prison sentences. He was determined not to be identified in any way, and that US bounty on his head made him extremely careful. He noted the size and audacity of some criminal groups made them vulnerable.

He had originally entered Western Australia from South Africa carrying legal amounts of cash, but also hidden gold and diamonds. He had been aided and abetted by criminals at both ends, aided by favours for previous transactions. Corruption in Johannesburg had not been difficult to discover but the connections at each end were the things most valuable.

Patience and confidentiality were his major virtues. A small indulgence was owning a Harley Davidson motor bike which gave him the luxury of riding free in the open country around Victoria. He was a fitness freak and used membership in a gym as a casual and used his own building's gym regularly too. He valued time spent 'doing nothing'—yet, at the same time, he could never truly 'let it all go.' At no time now was his life ever uncontrolled. Quite the opposite, as his strength in financial investment meant that every day his net worth increased and required much thought. He was now quite wealthy.

On his arrival in Australia, Jon had set up several shell companies and invested in a number of businesses such as shoe manufacturing, optometric importing and wholesaling, that were legitimate registered local businesses. The shoe manufacturing was lucrative because he knew the business well and understood the need for skilled 'clickers' and machinists. These were mainly skilled new migrants who stuck together and could be motivated in ways Jon understood. Some violence was not unknown amongst them and knife skills seemed inherent.

Jon moved into protectionist activities in close-knit suburbs but always in the second or third person contact role. A favoured axiom was that "protection money is easier to collect than rates".

For a short period of time he dabbled in the black market, where everything worked with cash and operated from very early each morning. Supply and demand were the common criteria and that applied to many products and fringe players. He had some loose associations with bikie gangs, and soon earned a reputation for being tough and ruthless. Through third parties and quite anonymously, he branched into tobacco, drugs, guns, and human slavery. He wisely took his profits from these actions and quickly moved on. Discretion was among his better qualities and that kept him below the radar of both authorities and potential enemies. He moved into the much more refined area of drug importation; in particular cocaine and amphetamines which were easier to hide, package and transport.

Jon knew the absurd profits available, and was aware of the supply and demand cycles, and the excessively high prices achieved both for wholesale importation and even retail sales. It took time and patience to achieve supplies from Columbia and Mexico. Bought for as little as under A$1000 per kilo, Columbian cocaine had a street value 200 times as much. Ice at around A$400 to produce was equally as profitable. Alternative supplies from Mexico could fill any gaps. He noted that 70 percent of drug consumption was in NSW.

He was careful never to be seen as 'greedy', always expressed appropriate thanks, kept super-confidentiality, and always dressed at a sensible level—never showy or in a manner to attract special attention or envy. He owned a small dog, which he walked regularly in the nearby park, occasionally hiring a discreet walker when he was away for more than a day. The dual-key locks ensured that access only to the small separate part of his apartment was possible, and strictly adhered to.

Chapter 13

DI Linda Alexander
Bozo the Clown Case

In Melbourne, Detective Inspector Linda Alexander found it frustrating that there was still no obvious suspect for the murder of the 'clown' deposited in the Fitzroy Gardens. Not a whisper of a lead. All circus or carnival personnel were apparently accounted for and no missing fancy dress costumes had been reported.

Linda and Beth and the rest of the team discussed possibilities endlessly. Could DNA not turn up some leads? But searches made to date had made no connections. For logical reasons, it had been assumed that the 'clown' had a circus connection and also perhaps Romany connections? That was able to be quickly discounted by checking with those small communities in Australia.

Routine notices had been sent to the Australian Federal Police and all interstate connections. More as a long-shot, notices were also sent to the FBI, CIA, Interpol, and UK police. The description of a missing middle-aged Caucasian brought forth no responses. Hundreds of ideas, leads and any potential candidates for carrying out the bizarre murder, and the possible location of the murder, of the unidentified body were discussed. It made sense to consider the usual basics of 'who, when and why' but this had got them nowhere, and the usual suspects related to violent killings, such as the Aryan Brotherhood, various motorbike gangs, the Italian Mafia, turf wars over drugs, prostitution, people smuggling, and even enquiries into international money laundering, or unpaid debts, all brought them nil results. Consideration was even given to known 'crazies', but was discounted due to the sophistication demonstrated in the job. The illicit tobacco trade was considered but discounted after discussions with the relevant local taskforce. It had become accepted by the team that the murder had been at least a two-person job.

The biggest issue that frustrated Linda, Beth, and the whole team was their inability so far to identify the body. Who was this man? And following closely on that question, what was the motive? There was no particular message they could determine in the decapitation of a middle-aged Caucasian male, and the attached note had led them nowhere. There were no clues of any type for his reason to be! A local crime 'Mr Big' was given attention and visited, but it was deemed no connection seemed logical for the involvement in this murder of white-collar crime, importing and wholesaling of drugs, or the much bigger world of international crime syndicates.

Chapter 14

Aron Brodsky, Bounty Hunter

The myth (or was it the truth?) in NYC's more unsavoury areas about a bounty in existence on the head of a prominent family's missing member was often alluded to by local Melbourne heavies with US connections wanting to earn a small fortune. But often would-be bounty hunters found preliminary enquiries were difficult, deemed unlikely to succeed and thus they did not proceed.

One not so easy to dissuade was an underworld professional hitman living in New York City who had grown up in the mid 1950s with hardness and bitterness indelibly built into his makeup. He was a ruthless and successful bounty tracker. His name was Aron Brodsky. His initial approach was received by the Codonas' appointed family committee, who then arranged for him to speak to a law firm in NYC set up in relation to the bounty on the missing Hans. Every possible help in the form of connections and details was given to Aron Brodsky, including the opinion that Canada, Europe, Africa or even Australia could be possibilities and that the missing son may even be back involved in circus life.

The closeness of Canada made it the easiest first choice to Brodsky, who pursued all his connections vigorously, but to absolutely no avail. Second choice was Europe with no results either, but a rumour of the possibility of South Africa reached Brodsky. Further investigations took place over time with cash changing hands, and finally suggested Melbourne, Australia. Brodsky had no personal contacts there but it was easy enough to call in the names of connections from past history with his many cash distributions.

The wrong reaction was achieved. The undercover enquiries by Brodsky finally reached the ears and rang the alarm bells of the 'listening post'/agents that Jonathan Smith had set up in Chicago. They reported that Brodsky was a man of formidable energy and a highly skilled hitman known for his perseverance. The advice to Jonathan was that they believed this man had absolutely no information about any new identity created as yet—but he was on his way to Melbourne very well-funded, and was a professional with past successes under his belt. His mission was to kill the son, earn the bounty, and disappear back to the US.

Aron Brodsky made a mistake arriving in Australia himself. He arrived in Sydney, booked into a small old-fashioned pub in the Rocks area, and quietly started to work underground, but soon attracted underworld attention as an 'outsider' American asking questions and spending cash on enquiries. He thought he was making discreet enquiries about circuses and circus people, but all he managed to do was to attract attention for others to take his money. He would have been better to employ a local to dig around for him.

The Codona family tracked his progress through Sydney and received reports back from him on his progress, but so too did the appointed Chicago agent, acting for Jon in Melbourne, who was thus able to follow Brodsky's progress.

When Brodsky moved on to Melbourne carrying on in much the same fashion as he had done in Sydney, word filtered back to Jon Smith about the hitman. Jon sent a message back through the various levels of his 'grapevine' to his agent in Chicago to enact plan B, which was to eliminate Brodsky.

That required serious and discreet planning by the Chicago end. Not least because a message needed to be sent to the Codona family to back off the bounty! Jon also could be very vindictive. Questions to be considered were: local or imported hitman? Apparent accident or obvious hit? Poisoning by drugs, or physical violence? Who needed to be the perpetrator who would most likely be caught, or did it matter? Did Jon want the hitman/bounty hunter to simply disappear, or should there be a message, bold and clear back to his employer the Codona family, to drop the vendetta?

What about local police reaction?

The best advice Jon received was to use a local bikie gang and arrange it through an overseas crime syndicate, as far offshore as possible. So, in line with his motto of trying to keep it all as simple as possible, he put the wheels in motion to activate the killing through a long trail back through his agent in Chicago. Money was not to be a problem, and the basic outline was simple to establish.

Firstly, the murder needed extreme secrecy, and secondly, speed and simplicity. Other criteria, to form a message, included that the body was to be dressed and made up as a clown. No-brand clothing could be purchased offshore in, say, Hawaii or similar location, and posted to Australia just to cause confusion. Brodsky's body was to be left in an inner-city location and stripped of any personal identifying material. The plan included that the nature of the killing—the violence and unusual cadaver and clothing—was likely to make some international news services, hopefully including NYC.

It was all to evolve using an international crime syndicate and their connection to the most suitable local Australian motorbike gang, who could be secretly involved in the scheme. The financial rewards were to be substantial, involving cash and drugs, and all information was to be confined to only the two most senior leaders of the gang. The rewards included a mix of substantial cocaine cut from a 'block', amphetamines, a large amount of untraceable cash up front, and later significantly large bonuses for completing the job undetected.

High-level research conducted offshore resulted in not the biggest bikie gang being selected, but a small, vigorous, ambitious and tightly controlled smaller local gang.

Chapter 15

Hit on The Hitman

Aron Brodsky was not hard to find in Melbourne. Just as he had in Sydney, he attracted attention as an 'outsider' asking questions, while based in a small apartment just off Exhibition Street in the CBD. The motorbike gang 'boys' used for the job, although based in greater Melbourne, drew no notice as they sussed out his regular daily habits in the centre of the city. Brodsky did not ever notice them, even when on occasions when they had a beer in the same Irish pub bar. At the point the bikies came into the picture, Brodsky was making absolutely no headway on his search for Hans.

As part of their normal precautionary behaviour, the bikie gang's two leaders always called one another by the pseudonyms Jim and Jake. Probably unnecessary, but this job was a murder, with some bizarre conditions to fill, and they did not the chance of letting slip their real identities. The clown makeup would require some special knowledge; fitting the clown clothing on they considered would be a doddle. Finding the necessary premises to carry out the job could be a challenge. But it was not to be so, as it turned out. An old garage in a warehouse destined to be demolished in an older inner northern suburb in Melbourne was deemed perfect. No neighbours and no bright lights.

Two of the gang needed to be involved for the associated actions, not the least being when the body was to be moved across town to the Fitzroy Gardens. They also needed help in learning how to do a reasonable-looking job with the clown's face; that expertise, they decided, could be drawn from a random pickup in a Fitzroy pub giving them the rudimentary basics on how to apply facial makeup and bold lipstick.

The site for dumping the body had been chosen to maximise the publicity for the murder, to attract lots of media attention. The only other stipulation was to affix a note to the body of Brodsky. The intent was to connect as obviously as possible to a circus association.

The grabbing of Brodsky by Jim and Jake on the footpath outside the Irish pub went without notice or difficulty. No noise, no protestation: one quick blow to the midriff made it look as if Brodsky was slightly inebriated, and then being assisted to a (just stolen) rental car by the kerb. After knocking him unconscious in the car, they moved quickly to the warehouse, where the murder and decapitation was completed.

The detail required for treatment of the body was clearly known and included stripping every possible means of identification from the body. The job was gruesome even for hardened bikies, as decapitation was extreme, but the huge upfront payment already received and the future incentives helped assuage any concerns. Jim and Jake had been instructed to use gloves throughout the process and had been clearly informed that any mistakes would see them cut adrift with no support. The two were not without experience in serious violence, and under no illusions as to the possible outcomes for them if anything went wrong. But the incentives were huge. They set about the job in hand to transform the body of the 'Yank' into something else; a bloody silly-looking circus clown! Amid the serious endeavour Jake could not help himself from commenting to Jim, "We are a couple of bloody clowns ourselves!"

The reality of what they were doing in the warehouse was not lost on either of them; as hardened criminals of around 35 years of age they were about to hit a golden prize in their somewhat ugly existence—or they could end up in jail, or even dead themselves. They cracked on with the task at hand and soon had the highly decorated cadaver in a big black body bag. They had handled them before. The warnings about gloves and wiping down all surfaces were well remembered and diligently carried out.

Transporting the body in the middle of the night was a logistical challenge, and required the use of the stolen rental car and also a motorbike which they had previously deposited at the warehouse, to make their escape after dropping off the body. The two vehicles arrived at the Fitzroy Gardens, and the challenge of remaining unnoticed as they moved the body across the Gardens, which were well-lit in parts, seemed to go ok. They quietly traversed the area, which at 2am appeared totally empty. The body-toting pair seemed to attract no notice in spite of Jack constantly cautioning "Shush, shush."

Arriving by the decorative pond by the Conservatory, they unceremoniously dumped the body, checked the note remained in place, and with controlled haste left on the bike, leaving no tracks.

Chapter 16

Aron Brodsky: Who is He?

The long arm of the law often moves in mysterious ways.

The New York Police Department (NYPD) had been notified and thus became interested in the apparent absence of one of the better-known ruthless underworld figures, named Aron Brodsky. He was known as a professional bounty hunter and hitman for hire, and rumour had it that he not been heard of for three months or more. An alert NYPD officer sighted the VicPol memo from Melbourne and exchanges began. It took a while but Linda, Beth and the pathologist became more confident that Brodsky could be their man.

No wonder the body was so hard to identify. Brodsky had disappeared from his usual haunts in New York some months ago, and had last been noticed in Canada, where it was rumoured he was onto some new and lucrative contract. The same rumour mill suggested he had gone on to Europe on a special mission. Putting two and two together, Linda's team concluded that the 'big shot' who had landed in Sydney then went on down to Melbourne, but now seemed to have disappeared suddenly from there, could be Aron Brodsky. They wondered why he had been asking so many questions? He was by nature a loner and that protected him in some ways from other criminals.

They concluded that he had not known at this stage where his target was or what identity he was using. The money he splashed around had not done the trick, neither had his digging connected to circuses. The questions remained for the police: "Who was he, and why? Who had left the note on the body? What did it all mean?"

There really were no further leads at this moment. The team concluded that a one or two, or even a three-person team must have been required. They would have needed premises and vehicles. Linda requested permission to fly to New York to meet with NYPD senior detectives to find out more about Brodsky.

Firstly, Brodsky was known as a loner so unlikely to have recruited extra help in the US. He would only have received information for himself. Secondly, the way he had splashed money around in Australia for information, it seemed unlikely he was sure of the location or current identity of the target.

Linda's enquiries in NYC revealed Brodsky had possibly been attracted to a slightly mysterious bounty reward for carrying out a 'hit' on a member of a prominent circus family. Try as they might the local NYPD (along with the FBI with all their resources) could not make the slightest crack in the wall of secrecy and protection surrounding the matter. The only relatively solid information that came to light was that it seemed the matter went back many years and was somehow connected to circus life.

Nothing more was identified. Linda promised to send some DNA material that could be useful. She returned home virtually empty-handed, but with more personal connections to USA law enforcement. Meanwhile, Beth and her team were still busy searching for motives and murder location. Police pathology was still focusing on searching for identity.

Back in Melbourne, Linda was determined to positively identify the mysterious Aron Brodsky. Through Beth and her team's detailed doorknocking of every hotel, known accommodation places and local coffee shops, they arrived at a rough picture of his style and habits. He listened to CNN international news and often quoted that source at the bar of the local Irish pub. If not having a beer, he drank a two-shot dark bitter coffee, no sugar. He had been sighted in black clothes and a black singlet; no tattoos visible. Enquiries indicated he seemed to have no contacts, friends or relations in Victoria.

The accommodation he had rented for cash in central Melbourne was soon discovered and turned over for anything that could help identify Brodsky. Cash, drugs and amphetamines were found, thought to have been used by him for influence.

Almost by chance, but due to relentless police pressure and enquiries, the owner of the old warehouse in North Melbourne reported a break-in and damage, and concern about what looked like dried blood on the floor. A bright young constable thought it could be relevant to the case, and neighbours were spoken to but had seen or heard nothing. However, the eventual inspection resulted in alarm bells back to Linda and so Beth and her team went to inspect. After DNA testing—voila! The first real lead.

Again: Why? The more questions they asked, the more the answers seemed to them that Brodsky had been to be a loner underworld figure who had arrived in Australia convinced that he had an opportunity to collect a huge bounty. He had no associates in Australia or the US, and his only connection seemed to be to a circus family in NYC. Linda and the team started to pull all the threads together.

Chapter 17

The Trail

The forensic inspection of the North Melbourne warehouse revealed evidence of recent occupation and activities, despite bikies Jim and Jake being meticulous in the cleanup. Most revealing was a connection to motor bikes.

Testing of the substance on the floor proved it was blood and it belonged to the deceased Aron Brodsky, but there was nothing else, except some oil drops—possibly from a motor bike? A stolen rental car was reported days later containing traces of what looked to be hair, skin and blood, and some upholstery damage. The blood belonged only to Brodsky and no one else. A pattern was building up.

Linda sent the details off to her contacts at the NYPD and also the FBI, to confirm if it was Brodsky, and advised them they had no known Australian connections here.

Linda also conferred with her superiors about the best action to take from here. The decision was made to maintain absolute concentration on the local scene to establish motive. Motorcycle gangg members notorious for lack of cooperation were to be targeted for even the smallest possible crack in the wall of silence. Someone with a modicum of makeup skill had been responsible for the clown makeup on Brodsky: it was decided to advertise widely for possible involvement, with a reward offered for information.

But unsurprisingly it seemed the motto of the bikies was, 'Hear no evil, see no evil—there is no evil!'

The request for help from the public, and perusal through CCTV footage provoked equal nil results. The protagonists had disappeared. In simple terms, the likely villains were beyond speculation. Huge police pressure was brought to bear on the motorbike fraternity— both clubs and gangs. There had to be serious money in circulation, and Linda and Beth pulled every lever they knew within their own and other police departments, undercover agents and the AFP. Major media was asked to refresh and refocus on 'The Clown' murder event. Superintendent Brunton was constantly in touch with encouragement and regularly attended strategy meetings held by Linda and Beth. And finally a possible breakthrough: a young blonde-haired hairdresser called into the Police Station in Fitzroy and very hesitantly reported she may be able to help and hoped not to be in trouble!

In her words, "A few weeks ago, my girlfriends and me were picked up in a pub in Fitzroy—the Everleigh—by a couple of guys we didn't know but they seemed OK, and their major interest was whether or not one of us was a makeup specialist. They bought us a couple of drinks. They were in their thirties, clean shaven, and offered us cash and drugs. They were called Jim and Jake. None of us were cosmeticians, so they moved off. We think they had motorbikes."

The renewed media publicity being given to the headless victim, or 'Bozo the Clown', seemed to be resonating. The best of the information was that 'bikies' were involved. Undercover police went into top gear looking for anyone flush with cash or drugs showing off a bit. But not a whisper or rumour was to be found. Linda and Beth were again very frustrated and becoming more and more irritable with the lack of progress.

As often happens, a little luck can change everything, and more detailed searching turned up several small pieces off a motorcycle found by a pathway in the Fitzroy Gardens. Experts were able to identify them as from the handlebars of a Harley Davidson Electra glide bike, which included a 100th anniversary badge and part of a broken plastic wing from close to the fairing frame.

Harley Davidson experts were convinced the pieces came from a TC88 model. Opinion varied as to whether the pieces found around the park could have been broken actually in the park. No real opinion emerged as to whether the pieces came from a current model or a rebadged or rebuilt motorcycle. What it all meant to the police team was that evidence was building up giving them a direction to concentrate on. Now the team went into top gear to focus on the most likely members of a gang that could be likely culprits in such a diabolical scheme.

The big five or six bikie gangs seemed unlikely, as they had big overseas connections and mature leadership structures and only carried out large jobs. They, in general terms, were feared as strong enforcers and with total control of their own members. Therefore, a smaller, aspirational, locally-controlled gang with a penchant for criminal activities like drug dealing, smuggling, or extortion for their advancement was considered by Linda. Small and ruthless and membership by selection and invitation.

The combinations of false name initials and rebuilt Harleys proved quite difficult as usual for the Police to identify, as most bikie gang members did not use their own names and many bikes were real hybrids or reconstituted unregistered bikes.

In spite of all the possibilities and doubts, the constable in charge of researching any rewards for a murder was confident a raid on the premises of the 'Harriers' motor bike gang in the west of Melbourne would be justified. That proved to be true. After a huge police undertaking was approved and put into action, the range of results included false number plates, unregistered firearms, large amounts of cash, alcohol and some drugs. The hoped-for drugs that may have been associated with such a large raid were not in evidence. The two most senior members of the club seemed to merit further possible attention. They were taken into custody amid loud protests and a demand for their lawyer to be present. Much pressure and outlines of possible charges that could be laid were exaggerated before the two were released. At the same time they were being detained, a uniformed police team was planning another raid on the club premises looking for further evidence or information—money, drugs, associations, even information on new spending. Simple pressure! Other enquiries were made on members of other bikie gangs, who were known to leak information to police on rival clubs when it suited them.

The crack in the armour came through information passed on from an informer. A hairdresser in Broadmeadows named Tereza had expressed her disbelief to the informer about a story one of her other customers had told her in amazement, that her bikie partner had stood her a full-on all-day spa with facials, massages, hairstyling etc, as he had come into a sudden big payoff.

Police followed up and spoke to hairdresser Tereza who, when pushed, told them about her local customer. Further information from the customer was that her boyfriend George had suggested she should also get a tattoo on her inner upper arm that said, 'I love GH', as she had announced to George that she was pregnant. He was George Hayward, a leader of the Harriers bikie gang.

Police research now flew into top speed. Hayward's co-leader was called Gerard Hodgkinson. Lower-level gang members were not aware of any gang involvement in the 'Bozo the Clown' murder, nor any knowledge of the scale of riches paid out in association with the event. Several bikes were taken away and the pieces found in or around the Fitzroy Gardens did seem to have come off a model similar to that claimed to be ridden by George Hayward. Further research indicated George had a long record with other gangs and a reputation for violence but was not considered overbright. His favourite saying was, "Now we are cooking with gas!"

George Haywood and Gerard Hodgkinson were taken into custody again and interviewed separately, with long periods waiting in isolation between interviews to add to the stress. Linda and Beth were to undertake the effort to crack their cast-iron alibis. They moved into full professional mode, which included a steady flow of uniformed members of their team entering and leaving the interrogation room with updated information.

Snippet after snippet of information was tabled. The 'good cop bad cop routine' was going nowhere until Beth broached the subject of children with George, and how a jail sentence would curtail any future family involvement. She added how much she enjoyed family life. When Linda finally suggested Gerard may get a lesser sentence, George began to crumble. The 'Jim and Jake' cover disappeared.

Superintendent Brunton kept up to date with proceedings and asked Linda, "Do you need help or additional expertise?" She thought not as there seemed to be no prior connection between the gang and Brodsky. That proved to be a comment of real wisdom, because George Haywood admitted he did not know Brodsky even though he and Hodgkinson had probably killed him 'by mistake' after being contacted through an associate they knew from the Casino. They had only been given the description of the person and 30 percent of a large payment up front. None of his gang were aware of any part of the 'contract' and the source had been totally anonymous, though was suggested to be part of an overseas syndicate. Neither man admitted to authorship of any note.

Chapter 18

Jonathan Samuel Smithson

It had taken time and dedication for Jon to remain below the radar of any form of detection or notice by law authorities. His companies and even low-profile associates were almost like ghosts. He was a cleanskin.

His methodology was simple. He was the owner-operator of all his activities, hidden behind an impenetrable wall of shell company organisations, with no favours owed or arrangements with anyone. His cash flow requirements could be boosted as needed by the simplest of all systems. He arranged through prior contacts illegal products to be brought in from Tanzania, Vietnam, Philippines and Thailand, in association with human traffickers; mainly gold secreted in their luggage or bodies. If they were apprehended by Customs and arrested, they were sent home but mostly the small goods they carried as mules got through in Australia. There were casualties but the attitude was, 'who cares'.

There were also diamonds from out of South Africa, a really good cash flow source as there were always desperate people in that nation willing to take their chances to make money.

For Jonathan there was no risk, no possible association with himself, and no loss as the source of the people or products was impossible to connect. A small registered importer, based in Williamstown, was no more than a post box cleared occasionally by a legal clerk from a respected city law practice. The mail was passed on to a staff member of a shell company out of Melbourne.

Jon and his arms-length activities came and went not quite by whim but more accurately as and when opportunities presented. Loan sharking and protection moves all came and went as more protected and sophisticated avenues evolved. Privacy and anonymity were a fundamental requirement. Mobile telephones and throw away 'burners' were becoming the more favoured communication method. Support equipment included cars, boats, machinery, hair and massage equipment, and kids' toys. It only required imagination —and often disguises.

Jon, being the loner he was, made no personal contacts. All his professional dealings were at arm's length to the extent of at least a third or fourth person. All his overseas transactions were handled through a variety of remote actions. Jon had had absolutely no connection with Brodsky, who was simply unlucky that his behaviour in Australia had set off a series of red flags that had been planted in a range of countries many years ago. The alarm had been sent back via a small, efficient, anonymous IT specialist in New York. It was no more than a collector of messages from around the world to pass on information. Interpretations of that information was delegated elsewhere. The end result was that Brodsky was eliminated with little fuss. The slightly quirky addition of the clown-look had been ordered by Jonathan as a surprise 'humourous' act and hopefully a warning to the Codona family.

In general terms, Brodsky could be described as an opportunistic hitman/bounty hunter. He was not from a traditional criminal background. He was just himself with no associates, family or friends. Very hard to catch.

At great arm's-length connections, Jon had access to organised international crime syndicates. He was very organised.

He actually lived in a 'cage' of his own making. He had no way out of it, even though in reality he could have almost anything he wanted. His current position in life had taken years of disguise and deceit to achieve, and it required huge concentration from him to record details of his fortunes held in Cayman banks, or Guernsey, and even the Solomon Islands.

Even in his desperate times, Jon had no trackable vices and seldom indulged in absolutely unrestrained behaviour. To his credit, he retained a sense of humour and through regular exercise and good luck was strong and healthy. One of his most enjoyable forms of relaxation was to put on a casual track suit and hoodie and walk around the beautiful Treasury Gardens just across the road from his safe apartment. Far from any trials and tribulations that could otherwise be a distraction.

Chapter 19

The Bikie Crims

George Hayward and Gerard Hodgkinson.

What a couple of losers! No real motive, no weapons, no morals, and no future.

Interrogation by the police was ruthlessly efficient, as the two suspected murderers seemed to be in ridiculous circumstances. They kept them in separate rooms and cautioned them officially with lots of added 'formalities'. Neither George nor Gerard had much experience with police tactics so did not recognise the time-wasting and distractions being put into effect by a series of different levels of uniformed police and detectives streaming in to ask the same type of questions over and over.

It was quickly established that George Hayward was the leader and Gerard Hodgkinson not much more than a dutiful follower. George disclosed he had not even discussed in detail what the full dollar amount of the job was, and what percentage of the 'fee' he was sharing with Gerard. Early on Gerard had whined, "It's nothing to do with me and I don't remember any details—I was high on a good hit."

Beth informed him in the most brutal manner, "A man has been murdered in an extraordinarily violent manner and we can locate you at the scene of the killing and the later depositing of the body in the park." She further outlined the likely sentence as being "jail for the rest of your life." He broke down and wept, and cried about his partner and child being deserted.

George was a different kettle of fish. He demanded his solicitor be present. This was arranged with help of an associate through his bikie gang and he refused to talk until such a person was present. Then the interrogation went back and forth over several hours without any progress. He was not rattled when Linda informed him of the mountain of evidence that had been gathered and the confession from Gerard, that he, George, was second in charge in the bikie gang but that the two of them had been independent of the gang in carrying out the killing of the clown. This had been 'their baby' and it was going to make them individually rich. Gerard had thought that there was nothing wrong with their motives as they had both been prepared to share with their girlfriends!

Chapter 20

Linda's Visit to US and a Link to Codona Family

The police in Melbourne were becoming sure that Brodsky was from New York City. *Almost* definitely. Previous information sent from Melbourne to the NYPD established that Brodsky or someone of a similar name was indeed known to them. DI Linda Alexander and DSS Beth Jenkins were authorised to fly to NYC to liaise with the NYPD in attempting to establish details of what Brodsky had been doing in Australia.

They were met at John F. Kennedy International Airport by NYPD Sergeant Max Llewellyn, a wonderfully friendly host. He took them to their accommodation and suggested to them that they be picked up the following morning at 8am. He checked if they had brought the identifying information and DNA. The answer was yes.

Fresh and enthusiastic, they regrouped the next morning and were introduced to many NYPD staff members, some of whom were really keen to meet 'genuine' Australians, even if Linda was from a South African background. It was easy to confirm the corpse in Melbourne belonged to someone who used the name Brodsky (or similar) and was known to the NYPD. He was around fifty years of age, had a record of misdemeanours over many years, ranging from standover tactics to serious burglaries. In more recent years a little more affluent, he lived in a city apartment and seemed to aspire to greater things. He did not appear to mix with a gang or special friends but did drink in a local hotel. Local information gathered revealed that he had been heard to say he was on to some form of bounty or treasure hunt. He had no known female friends or other companions.

On the second day Beth received a call from Melbourne saying one of her children had been hurt in a non-life-threatening but serious accident, so with regret Beth chose to hurry back to her home. With approval from Superintendent Brunton, Linda chose to stay on to pursue more about Aron Brodsky.

She found out he had grown up and was educated in New Jersey but had no identifiable companions from school. Like many lesser educated criminals who had 'streetsmarts', he had mainly kept out of trouble. From questions asked at his local pub it was found he had been boasting about a large reward for a job he was pursuing. The implied 'job' was to find a long-lost member of an American circus family. The last anyone had heard from him was that he was off to meet the family to receive more details.

Low-level non-inquisition type questions about any connection between Brodsky and the circus world or clowns specifically received puzzled looks and flat, 'bloody unlikely' responses.

Linda was finding the whole range of 'facts' quite fanciful.

Research into local clubs and hot spots failed to turn up any confirmation of large uncollected rewards for a missing person from times gone by. Persisting with that line through talking at length to a few dodgy legal firms, Linda was finally told there may be a connection to a suggested legal company in New York—which could be the only remote chance of a connection.

She lost the plot a little as her daily companion, Sergeant Max Llewellyn, with his great American-Irish sense of humour and deep

NYPD experience, was proving to be both interesting and infuriating. Working closely with him was becoming quite an issue for Linda, particularly as he was showing her he was having such an enjoyable time hosting the highly ranked police officer from Australia. Linda was flattered by the attention and respect she was receiving. Two days of intensive local underworld enquiries finally led them to a small legal practice where an anonymous elderly partner finally confessed, in high confidence, that he may be able to throw some light on the subject. In short, he admitted there were rumours of a reward (bounty) placed with them years ago by a New York circus family to find a member of their family who had absconded with family 'wealth'. As far as he knew, the bounty had never been collected.

Could Brodsky have been on the trail of the absconded person? The old lawyer thought not, as they had had no communication to that effect. But with assurances of confidentiality all around, he volunteered to make enquiries. That was OK for Linda and Max, and they did a little sightseeing together as they continued enquiries.

During their time together Linda would occasionally look up to see Max's dark brown eyes probing deeply into her light blue eyes. When she caught him doing it, she would ask, "How are we doing, mate?" Always the happy answer, "Never better Ms." They both smiled and enjoyed the moment. Even with the help of the NYPD and undercover divisions their enquiries ran out of time and last-ditch searches in areas born of desperation, such as social organisations like AA or similar, turned up no results.

With her return to Melbourne looming, Linda still had high hopes they may yet turn up a lead. On their last night together in New York, they consumed a range of alcoholic drinks to celebrate their efforts and somehow, they finished up in bed together. Linda was aware of her body trembling all over with excitement like a mild fever. She could not process any deep thoughts as she enjoyed the super-hot feelings, and they had the most enjoyable sex either had experienced for many months. Linda's partner Jack Classen in Melbourne was forgotten in the moment.

At the last minute, information turned up by the elderly lawyer they had seen suggested the name of Codona, a circus family who may be a contact. Linda flew home with a guilty conscience and a possible lead to Brodsky.

Chapter 21

Linda: So Sorry

Back in Australia, Linda's first call was to her friend and close Vic Police associate, Beth Jenkins. A really urgent call for a 'coffee meeting'. The get-together was like a confession, a call for guidance and support. Beth was a good philosopher and could crank out succinct sayings when appropriate. When she initially understood the level of drama and crisis involving her friend, her best contribution was a saying attributed to Leonard Cohen, "There's a crack in everything, that's how light gets in". She was a good listener and there to support.

Linda opened their talk by saying, "Beth, I need your help."

After hearing the story of the encounter in NYC, Beth then began asking questions; the basics really, "Was it a one-night stand, is he married, do you crave to see him again, is he a partner you would be proud to introduce to your friends and family? Is he debt free emotionally and financially? Has he any children reliant on him?"

All Linda could respond with was, "I don't know!" She admitted that the week or more together had stirred long-forgotten feelings of sexual freedom, warmth and emotion, and she 'perhaps' wanted to see Max Llewellyn again, which would probably eventuate as the case would require another visit to the law firm in NYC. They talked for ages, with Linda conscious she had ended a prior engagement quickly after meeting Jack. Beth suggested perhaps a letter or note of explanation to Jack could be a wise step? Seeking an understanding? An explanation? An apology? Did she want to continue with Jack?

After much reflection and consideration, Linda hand wrote the following:

'Dear Jack, I write this to say I'm so sorry. While away on my recent USA police trip, I slept with a close associate. What can I say? —please forgive me for this selfish act of betrayal that you do not deserve. I have been totally self-absorbed in my work recently, and have let you and your trust down. I hope some of the following can present some glimmer of light on my selfish behaviour.

Our two jobs require a heavy reliance and premium on trust and integrity, and this makes me even more humble in writing in an attempt to add some reason for my lapse. Family, genuine friends and our trusted loved ones are few and far between, and our work-obsessed personalities add their own pressure within the type of work we do.

Police work and culture is heavy going and not much 'fun'. Our life together has become quite lonely, and some silly light-hearted fun has become more difficult to enjoy together. A comfortable life but not exciting. Maybe it is the next stage of a relationship, or even the equivalent of middle-age boredom, or maybe more likely a character fault of mine? Are we to break up? Whatever the reason, I plead guilty. I have not yet given a thought to how my friends and yours would view our possible breakup. As you know, Beth is a close friend of mine, in fact my only real confidante, and I have spoken with her about this, but only in a superficial way.

Please read with patience my plea for understanding. People I care about have become more distant and that gives me a regular reminder of how isolated I feel. Some of that can easily be laid at my own door, as I have been accused of arrogance that can be associated with holding positions of authority and success early in life. I'm now well over 30 years of age and that gives me work status but not many close friends. You know my group of friends is very small. Loyalty has its limits and I feel so wretched that I may never see you again. We have grown less intimately personally, and I do not enjoy our nights together of watching silly TV.

Jack, this all comes with a huge apology and a plea to absorb my heartfelt emotions asking for your forgiveness. Let's talk in a couple of weeks as I need to return to NYC for one more followup of the major case I'm involved in. I really do love you but I can understand my behaviour has shattered your trust. You have always been a great companion and a true friend. We have both prided ourselves on sharing the truth together, and this hurts me having to make this admission of disloyalty. Why am I so needy? Just writing to you brings torrents of tears to my eyes.

As I began this note with 'so sorry', I finish in the same manner, I am so sorry. Forgive me.

Linda."

When she had finished the letter, her hand shook as she thought about how she could pass it on to Jack without breaking down into tears and hysteria. She talked it all over again with best friend Beth, who carefully explored her feelings for Jack (whom Beth knew) and asked more about 'the man from New York'. The stress of all this made Linda feel physically ill.

She told Beth his name, Max Llewellyn, and added he must be good with a name like that, and laughed nervously, trying to shake off her feelings of guilt and depression. She felt absolutely pathetic as she talked about him in more detail. To Beth, he did sound genuine and real but they had had only a short time together.

Beth added that it was going to be much more a matter of how deeply the damage had been done to Jack once he knew. With much heartache and more tears, Linda decided to mail the letter to Jack and to proceed with the trip back to the US, as her professional responsibilities must be carried out. She now realised that she lived in a job that controlled her life, and that was important to her. She could do most of the things she enjoyed, but perhaps there was to be no real personal happiness, no in-depth love history, no children? Then, as she often said to herself—with a nudge from Beth—"Don't beat yourself up!"

Jack received the letter and, amazingly, seemed not to be angry. He hid any hurt he felt and accepted the end of the relationship, saying merely, "We are all human and make mistakes. Now we must move on. Let's try to remain friends."

Chapter 22

US: More About Brodsky

Connection to Codona Circus

With a heavy heart and feelings of guilt, Linda two weeks later returned to the US. Her trip was given the blessing of Super. Ron Brunton, who in turn had elicited help from his equivalent rank in the AFP to arrange further assistance for Linda in the NYPD. The main reason was to arrange for her to meet discreetly with a senior lawyer in an international company law specialists firm named Elsner and Sommer. The rumour was that they had been instrumental in setting up and handling the 'famous' bounty on the life of a family member on behalf of the Codona Circus family.

The police officer appointed to help knew of the senior lawyer and was happy to arrange the meeting and accompany Linda to meet a Mr Daniel Cohen, of Elsner and Sommer in New York City. Daniel was warm in his welcome to this Australian Detective Inspector. He was interested in the reasons for the visit and sympathised with the many points advanced. When specifically asked, "Can you help us to understand the existence of such a reward?" His answer was, "Perhaps."

When further asked, "Can you, or will you elaborate with names of the ultimate provider/client of yours, or names of people you have provided with bounty information?"

His answer was an emphatic, "No!"

Linda then asked, "How about some information that might help us solve a very grisly murder?"

This met with a large smile and, "Perhaps, try me!"

Linda went on to explain that Melbourne Police had recovered the murdered body of a person named Aron Brodsky. Would Mr Cohen confirm that person was one to whom he had given details? The response was a guarded, "Possibly."

The main reason for the meeting was to try to establish the details behind Brodsky's motivation. What was the bounty dollar figure, and who was the target? Yes, Brodsky was a real person of Russian or Ukraine heritage, with no known criminal record. Daniel Cohen then gave a wry smile as the meeting nearly concluded.

With a lot of charm and encouragement from Linda, and assurances of total confidentiality from the police, he gave up a tiny concession, "It's a long time ago, it involved much confidentiality; the Codona Circus family was involved as the client, and the reward still exists but there has been no recent enquiry, except from your named person."

Linda admitted to Mr Cohen that Melbourne police wanted to confirm the reason for the murder. Assurances of complete co-operation were given.

Back at NYPD HQ, Linda was seriously taken aback by the presence of Max Llewellyn! His quick explanation was that a social evening had been arranged to exchange facts. While it was planned to be purely a further exchange of information, for Linda in particular it was a chance to assess her very personal feelings. Linda quickly found that she was still attracted to Max and so enjoyed the communications. There was no intention to have another intimate evening but the pleasure of meeting him again reinforced feelings.

Chapter 23

Linda and Melbourne Research

Cordona or Codona?
Family relationships and background

There is some confusion between the family names of Codona and Cordona in the US. The Codona family is smaller and was established in the US around 1920. They came from a long line of Gypsy circus families going back to both Romanian and Scottish/ Irish ancestry. Throwing more confusion into the mix in the US is the name 'Cardona' which has Spanish/Catalan heritage.

Hanzi/Hans aka Jonathan Samual Smithson's parentage was Codona from a Romanian circus background. Aron Brodsky had no connection: He was simply an opportunist hitman, but considered a professional heavyweight.

Using every authority known to Linda and her police associates, it was possible to slowly extract further details from lawyer Daniel Cohen and confirm that the 'bounty' was indeed in place from the circus family of the name Codona. As Cohen was the senior partner in the long-established law firm, he was made the decision to confirm that the family member the bounty hunter was seeking was named Hanzi, and that he had done a runner on family and friends and completely disappeared with family wealth. The senior family members had been shattered. More importantly, they planned revenge because of unique personal family circumstances as well.

Police work became easier now, because the Codona name was one of the most famous names in circus history. The Codona family themselves were famous as trapeze acrobats, artists and clowns. Daniel Cohen confirmed the Codona family was still very well known because of the various family acts still together and a past full of tragic events and sadness, with the most famous being the love of Lilian Leitzel and Alfredo Codona. The 'Flying Codonas' were rightly known all round the world for their death-defying acts. As members of the Ringling Brothers Circus, they toured worldwide, including performing in Australia. Tragedy followed. Alfredo had style and was exceptionally daring, performing the complex triple aerial somersault. Both he and Lilian were superstars of the circus, and both temperamental. Lilian fell when part of her rigging split, and she died from the injuries sustained. After a while, Alfredo returned to trapeze flying and married fellow aerialist Vera Bruce. But he had become reckless and later tore shoulder ligaments, ending his career. Vera eventully sued for divorce. Brother Lalo continued the act until torn muscles forced his retirement also. Risks and tragedies were all part of life in Codona history.

Lilian Leitzel had been memorable, as she was only four feet nine inches tall (about 145cm) and well known for her demanding personality. She was known to slap helpers—her temper was legendary. The other side of her personality was that she was liked by children in the family, who affectionately called her 'Auntie Leitzel'.

The Codona family was devastated by her death. A year after the tragedy, Alfredo ordered a five-metre white marble statue titled 'Reunion'. Engraved with the words, 'In everlasting memory of my beloved Lilian Leitzel Codona.'

The marriage of Alfredo to Vera Bruce (of Australian parents, but born in Singapore) was never a huge success. They were married in a ceremony in conjunction with the Circus Fans Association Convention. It seemed to be more a marriage of convenience than affection. Then Alfredo had a bad fall into a net at Madison Square Garden and tore his shoulder ligaments and his flying days were over. Over several years and occupations, Alfredo declined into a mundane lifestyle and Vera filed for divorce. Alfredo pleaded no contest and Alfredo and Vera Bruce met in the office of her attorney, James E Pawson in Long Beach, to finalise details of the settlement. It had been amicable. Alfredo told the lawyer that he wanted to be alone with his ex-wife. Pawson left the room and Codona drew a gun, shot Vera several times and turned the gun on himself. Alfredo died instantly and Vera the following day.

The tragedy was news all over the world, and was particularly devastating for circus performers. Vera Bruce-Codona was laid to rest at the Calvary Cemetery in Los Angeles with an inscription on the gravestone, 'Peace at Last.' A reputed suicide note found on the body of Alfredo Codona made a last request to be buried beside Lilian Leitzel Codona.

The tragedy was widely reported in the media and large crowds of circus colleagues and fans attended the funerals. Media coverage was summarised as, 'Love and Tragedy at the Circus.' What a volatile arena full of family dramas.

Chapter 24

The Brodsky Link

Linda and Beth were intrigued by the Codona family histories and how circus-oriented they were. They theorised about how Aron Brodsky had finished up from his bounty research to be in Australia.

The answer was probably both a very large fluke and leaks from connections. His research threw up the Codona family/Vera Bruce name and Ringland's Circus performing in Australia. It had not occurred to the bounty hunter that Hanzi had probably have changed his name and appearance. Would Hanzi really seek to be involved in circus life when he knew a reward would be put on his life by his furious father?

Linda had established from lawyer Daniel Cohen that the bounty still existed and it seemed there were no current applicants out looking for the target.

Linda was happy with the help and cooperation received from the NYPD and also the FBI and individual staff members, but to those authorities it was only low-key attention, as Brodsky was not high in their priorities. Even more so as the Codona son who had run away and disappeared had broken no local laws. Their interest was, in fact, close to nil.

The personal episode with Max Llewellyn was now a part of

life for Linda to cope with herself. It had been a surprise and an exciting interlude in her otherwise mundane personal life, but she and Max admitted there was no future possible. They'd stay friends and professional associates. In her own mind Linda resolved that apartment life as a loner and career woman was comfortable.

Linda and her whole team including DSS Beth Jenkins, supervised by Ron Brunton, discussed how to finalise the murder of 'Bozo aka Brodsky, the Clown'.

They had in custody the two bikies, 'Jim' and 'Jake' who were George Hayward (leader) and Gerard Hodgkinson. They were not much further use to anyone in terms of investigations, unless they could throw some light on any drug trafficking activities and bikie gangs, if indeed they possessed any further intelligence of value. However, Gerard was proving to be quite the whinger and giving out more information. It was decided to keep things simple for now, and proceed to trial.

Chapter 25

Melbourne
Two Lonely Souls

DI Linda Alexander.

She was not really lonely, just readjusting to life as a single. Her friendship with fellow officer Beth Jenkins was strong and at least once per week she telephoned or texted a greeting, "how's it going?" and then had an exchange of personal or professional rumour. They were able to trust one another.

Jack was now just a good friend and social companion, 'when and as required'.

One of Linda's favourite escapes was to wander around the Treasury Gardens and the Fitzroy Gardens, right across from the apartment she had now owned for over three years. The Kerekere Café with its own style of uncluttered friendliness, set among the beautiful mature trees, was a haven of peace and solitude. Lansdowne Street dissecting the two parks was a busy main road, but did not detract in any way from the unhurried calmness of the entire area. Captain Cook's Cottage, the River God Fountain, the miniature English Village, and the Fairy Tree all made it a magical place for quiet contemplation for Linda. The quietude was seldom broken by noisy children, loud tourists or protesters. When arranging with Beth for a walk together in the park and then a coffee in the café, they knew it would be quiet and a good place to walk and chat.

The size and complexity of illegal drug importations into Australia had grown exponentially in recent times. As a major part of Linda's responsibilities, the need for more and more specialised staff became inevitable. Police culture and its engagement with public relations entailed a range of complex obligations. One of Linda's memberships from a long way back was with the Carlton Football Club. She rather enjoyed some of the facilities and occasional use of the gym equipment. She had on occasions attended matches and was treated with respect. Such a membership with all the attention it could bring did her status no harm.

The force had a strong determination for officers to continue their education and maintain physical well-being. Compulsory attendance at the various police and other seminars was not so enjoyable for Linda. The high rank she had now achieved meant she was on occasions a key speaker at functions and asked to join a panel of 'experts' at others. Her life was very busy and full.

Her personal mantra was, 'What other people think is none of my business'.

Another real escape from work for personal relaxation was her participation in women's basketball. It was all very professional, being part of the Big V semi-professional league sport, with forty plus associations and one hundred and fifty teams. There were grades A to D and many juniors. Each team needed five players per game and additional backups. It was all great fun and there was much rivalry at all grades. Linda and Beth had been friends and team members together, both socially and as players, over many seasons. Their team was a police team and coincidentally the coach was Superintendent Ron Brunton, who had been a top League player in his youth. Linda and Beth played in Grade C with mainly current or retired members of the Vic Police, though work demands meant they often missed either training or matches. But morale was high and a number, including Coach Brunton, were part-time participants as their duties allowed.

Super 'Coach' Ron Brunton inspired a quiet dedication. As would be expected, team members were competitive and liked to win. They were noisy in their camaraderie with hugs and cheers and pats on backs. Beth was a great captain and respected as leader. It was fun, and offset some of the singlemindedness and serious focus associated with their jobs. Ron was held in great respect and praised by all as an important part of the team. He was friendly to all, but not a friend to anyone.

Great rivalry existed between teams in the grade and in particular between teams from the Ambulance and Fire Services—not ordinary services to the public. There was edge and 'aggressive banter' in barracking. The fierce rivalry that existed on court allowed a little extra push and shove. Ambos and Fireys—enemies on court but great comrades off court.

Team friendships overflowed from basketball and support was given when disappointments arose.

Jonathan Samual Smithson

Owner/occupier of his upmarket apartment in Spring Street, East Melbourne, the so-called 'Paris end' of town, and from any records that existed, Jon would be seen as the ultimate cleanskin. In fact, there were no adverse records on him at all. He was unknown and untraceable, and he had the system in place with his 'listening post' in Chicago by which he could be quickly warned if any red flags were raised and there were enquiries about his distant past as 'Hanzi aka Hans Codona', and act to create even more blocks.

On the good side of his present life, he had achieved genuine anonymity. This meant he had no claim or responsibilities to or from relatives, or any deep friendships in his past or current life. He had deliberately avoided making any regular close friendships. This was not hard with the need for constant lookout so indelibly stamped in his psyche. However, slowly, he had made several low-key friends and had begun to join a few social clubs, such as the Collingwood Football Club. This was not hard to do, with a number of appropriate existing club members acting as 'seconders' on any new application. With great care, he had involved himself in a few activities and had begun to attend matches irregularly, owned a Collingwood scarf and jacket, and even learned to sing the Club anthem.

He did not carry any guilt or consideration for the harm done to other human beings resulting from drug use. No conscience; he lived in strong survival mode!

Being now without any particular accent or behavioural actions, no one pressed him about his background. He always paid his way and never 'big noted'. His main vehicle was a basic Mazda car, deliberately chosen to keep himself inconspicuous.

Most of the time in the CBD he travelled by tram or taxi and always limited his alcohol intake to a comfortable level. His favourite haven, apart from his luxury apartment in the Spring Street high-rise complex, was the 78 acres of the adjacent beautiful green parklands of the two City gardens, where he would happily wander incognito. A favourite coffee stop was the Kerekere café in the Fitzroy Gardens (considered the jewel in the crown of Melbourne parks) situated opposite the beautiful Conservatory there. Another favourite spot was the Excello Café in Spring Street, opposite the Parliament. All close to his home for quiet, easy walks.

A much bigger step for him but still designed for ultimate non-recognition was the purchase of a small property in Malmsbury in central Victoria, an hour and a half on the Calder motorway northwest of Melbourne towards Bendigo. This property met the many criteria that Jon applied to his current decision-making. It was a slightly old-fashioned house on a little under half an acre, well fenced, and had a double garage facing the non-sealed road and mature trees on the property. All mod cons including electric gate and garage door. There was a not-too-close neighbour, who became a trusted 'friend', being a no-nonsense semi-retired handyman — known in the local pub as a Jack of all trades.

Jon's other indulgence was his second-hand Harley Davidson motor bike. When finalising the purchase he had said to the seller, "I intend to fly along enjoying the fresh air and freedom and to enjoy it all, such as the beauty of the fantastic viaduct near Malmsbury." He had in mind a visit or two to Lake Eppalock for more nefarious reasons, beautiful though it may be. He did not join a motorcycle club and nor did he anticipate taking friends or others as pillion passengers.

The different perspectives of two people looking at the same scenario; what each one sees and the benefits and pleasure they acquire from the same scenery is so varied.

DI Linda Alexander.
Linda's greatest pleasure was wandering around some of what are described by Melbourne Parks and Garden's promotional gurus as the 'Secret Walks of Melbourne Parks and Gardens'. She had enjoyed them now for years and not even the current case she was working on could spoil that enjoyment. The case took the nickname 'Bozo the Headless Clown' and despite its bizarre nature had been quickly forgotten by the public.

The two parks most relaxing for her were the smaller, at 14 acres and with a population of brushtail possums, the Treasury Gardens just across the road from her apartment, and the larger, more interesting and bigger gardens across Lansdowne Street, the Fitzroy Gardens, which totalled 64 acres and contained two kilometres of paved walkways; enough room for anyone seeking some privacy!

Linda, when seeking a relaxation break and dressed in trackie-style pants, T-shirt and runners, cap and sunnies, became almost unrecognisable. She was not flashy but neither was she trying to hide. For more strenuous exercise her apartment block had a full gym and pool. On occasions she met friends or associates for coffee in the KereKere café and in a leisurely way had enjoyed all the tourist spots too—Cooks Cottage, the Conservatory, Sinclair's Cottage, the Model Tudor Village, the River God Fountain, and of course the Dolphin Fountain plus the Avenue of Elms and hundreds of wonderful, ever-changing flowers.

When feeling more vigorous, adventurous, or with time available, she 'power walked' across to the Carlton Gardens and enjoyed the grandeur of these gardens and the World Heritage-listed Royal Exhibition Building with its famous dome architecture. Linda enjoyed the small social activities arranged by her building's body corporate committee, and regularly used the gym and pool when time was available. The body corporate committee knew she was a senior member of the Victoria Police force.

Jon Smithson

The current major concern for Jon was a much-filtered message originating from his confidential 'eyes and ears' in Chicago. A source had revealed that an unknown had registered interest with a firm of attorneys in New York City regarding full information and background around the bounty available for finding Hanzi Codona. Information available in general terms was that this applicant was number 14 over the many years, following Aron Brodsky No 13, who was over two years ago.

Jon was characteristically calm as he knew his precautions against any trail leading to him were absolutely watertight. His

Chicago agent was aware of the obtuse message attached to the demise of Brodsky, 'no more clowns; no more leaks!' Jonathan no longer ever in his mind related back to his original name of Codona, and it never entered his mind to check back to New Jersey in the US on any of his original family's health or welfare.

The enquirer number 14, who thought Brodsky may have had a significant lead on Jon, had been informed that the police in Melbourne were satisfied that the murder had been solved and the crime was local. Nevertheless the new hunter took it on himself to dig further and make a trip to Australia. His research was mainly about Brodsky who had a famous European Jewish background. No connections with the poet Brodsky and apparently no siblings. In Australia there was only a tiny number of people with the same name including a distinguished soldier who had been a respected Anzac. The new hunter spent time in Melbourne trying to quiz the police about circus employees and anyone named Codona or Cordona. They admired his persistence, as he even tried to penetrate the bikie gang from which Jim and Jake had graduated—who had recently been found guilty of the murder of Brodsky. That concluded the Melbourne investigations from enquirer number 14 for now.

Jon was mature enough to appreciate that different people saw the 'same' things in different ways—beauty is in the eye of the beholder. For Jonathan, nothing could be more accurate as he beheld the surrounds of his day to day life. He lived inside his security-tight apartment with personal pleasure. For fresh air he roamed freely outdoors but with care and disguise. For high level business meetings he blended perfectly with regular senior business types, doing what they did. He had early on worked out how to exit his building without the Concierge services noting he had gone.

His usual attire for outside roaming was a pair of slightly old but not raggedy trousers, shirt and jacket, shoes and socks, and sometimes gloves. He assumed a limp and carried a walking stick for effect, and protection if needed. Always with sunglasses and a cloth cap on, and his eyes constantly moved back and forth. Anyone from his business world would be hard pressed to recognise him.

Jon walked 'The Secret Parks and Gardens' route close to his apartment with great care and close observation. He viewed with enjoyment the Carlton Gardens, the Melbourne Museum, and the wonderful Moreton Bay fig trees. Sometimes he veered off along Nicholson Street into Albert Street by St Patricks Cathedral to admire the beautiful bluestone building. Most of these sojourns would bring him back into the Fitzroy Gardens, to a significant place there, his special haven, the Conservatory.

Although invited to participate on his building's body corporate committee or attend social events, or celebrations, Jon usually declined with thanks. The Concierge staff hardly recognised him and he never spoke to them on first name terms. He was totally nondescript and under the radar.

In one moment of unusual extravagance, Jon exchanged a few words with the Concierge that he had learned as a child from his mother. "Son, make sure the words that come out of your mouth are soft and sweet because some day you may have to eat them." He attributed the saying to a European relation.

Chapter 26

Meeting Jon

The apartment building in Spring Street was forty storeys high containing over 240 units. It was mainly owners living on site but there were some tenants in a minor number of units. Apartments ranged from the top floor penthouse, to all sizes through 1 bed and 1 bathroom, 2bed/2bath, 3bed/3bath, 4bed/4bath, all with balconies, and some with one car park and others with more. Pets were allowed with some size constraints.

An eclectic mix of accommodation, recreational privileges, personalities, behaviour, and integrity. There were monthly social functions such as drinks evenings, coffee afternoons, and weekly book clubs, Pilates, pool activities and bridge and mahjong meets. Occasionally, the body corporate committee also organised special functions in the main foyer to celebrate notable events and for those living in the building to get to know one another. It could be the annual event for the building's opening, or the festive season, or a major sporting event or even elections.

In general terms the building events were low key: no speeches, no congratulations, not much more than alcohol, snack food, and a good ambience. Most attendees were well dressed for the occasion and wore labels showing their unit number and first name. Easy to make a first conversation. A token charge of $20 each was charged for the one-to-two-hour functions. At the beginning of these events there was a constant flow of arrivals, some with big loud acknowledgements of recognition and others just looking for a friendly face. Some just huddled together and other more gregarious types loudly introduced themselves to anyone standing close by.

Jon usually declined all the social invites, but at last decided to attend one event and stay only a minimal time. He was an early arrival and recognised some of the 'serious' types who were on the body corporate committee, whom he had met briefly in the early days of his purchase. Friendly to them, but not friends. Jon knew no one well on a personal basis.

He was doing the usual routine chit chat at such social meetings, where information is exchanged on where have you been lately? What do you do? What shows or movies have you seen? as people try to be friendly. Some ask, "what do you do?" trying to find common ground. Holidays locally or abroad are common subjects, as are regional venues such as Daylesford, Meeniyan, Rutherglen, King Valley, Otway Ranges and Grampians; somewhere there is bound to be a common interest. Never too personal. All very pleasant.

Linda arrived around 6.30pm with a plan to just say "hello" to the few she knew, and those who knew she was a member of the police. Most had no idea of her police seniority. The evening progressed well until by coincidence, Jon and Linda were in a small group of six or so people chatting away, as they do when relaxed by a good ambience and in some instances a little alcohol. Both Linda and Jon had long ago learned to stick to non-alcoholic drinks at social functions. Inevitably, a loud and slightly coarse man directly addressed Jon, and in a bombastic way after looking at his name tag said, "Well Jon, what do you do for a crust?"

Quietly, Jon responded, "Not much really, as I am semi-retired these days, but I do as much as I can with what I have got."

That brought a wry smile to others in the group, as the 'loudmouth' then took the opportunity he wanted, to dive into his life in finance, superannuation, term deposits and the merits and otherwise of the banking system. He rattled along in his own glory until another member of the small group graciously asked, "Linda, I believe you are in the Victoria Police?"

Linda humorously replied, "Yes, name, rank, and pay level is all I'm allowed to disclose. And I'm not sure about the last item!" and as designed that got a good laugh.

The senior banking executive had one more shot of attention seeking by directly asking what he thought was a pertinent question of Linda, "Why do you think there are currently so many men assaulting women?"

She replied with a fierce tone, and a straight face right onto him, "Evil is an equal-opportunity employer!"

The little group began to break up and as Jon took his leave, Linda said in her usual forthright way, "I like your attitude, perhaps we could have coffee together some time. You should know I have no agenda! Good night," and away she went. She noted he seemed a few years older than her, had a quiet manner, and had an international accent, hard to place.

Everything can change in the blink of an eye.

Chapter 27.

Getting to Know You

It was true that neither of them had any idea of any possible connections.

DI Linda Alexander left for work at police headquarters around 6.30am Monday to Saturday. She had a team of assistants and one senior acting almost as a secretary. She was regimented by meetings at a variety of locations. She was respected as an early bird, leading her team from the front, even-tempered and available.

She was never particularly interested in the people at the social functions at her building, but in an idle moment, and for no apparent reason, she looked up within her police resources 'Jonathan Smithson'. No surprises; Australian citizenship from a background in South Africa, not married. A few years older than her and no police record.

Linda did not consider herself lonely, in fact she liked being on her own after a really busy work day. Regular conversations with Beth Jenkins and her family members in Western Australia were her comfort, support and protection. The only passing thoughts in her mind about Jonathan were that he seemed quite friendly though impersonal, and did not volunteer information, but seemed interesting enough. She would probably never meet him again. Her extensive police experience always channelled her thought processes down logical highways seeking contacts and information if relevant.

Jonathan, these days, considered his overall plan and comfort zone was to try to be 'different' but stay very low-profile. He tried to look at things from all angles, upside down and round-about, to get to the other side of reasons and opinions. Bizarrely, he often slept at night with his feet on the pillow and his head at the foot of the bed. He seldom stayed up late at night, and often arose at 5am and went for a walk around the local streets for a coffee. He knew which cafes opened up early enough and provided good coffee and croissants. He practised careful planning and excessive security.

It was to be months before Linda and Jonathan were to meet again. One morning in April around 6.30am, Jonathan was waiting in the foyer for a lift to take him back up to his apartment, and Linda exited the lift. She was in smart business clothes and Jonathan was in plain but practical garb.

After a perfunctory greeting, recognition then took a moment or two but finally succeeded. In a friendly way he said with a smile, "off to work?"

In an equally friendly manner, she posed her question, "Just home from work?"

He just smiled at her and said, "Have a really good day" before entering the lift. No further effort from him to engage. Linda spent the day reflecting on his quiet assurance and easy manner.

Their next encounter was only one week later, again in their building's foyer but this time it was a later time of day.

After initial, "hello, nice to see you again" and then a lapse in talk, in an extraordinary (for him) manner, Jon said, "You look just about bushed and I'm off to a late lunch at my favourite Café Excello just along the street; would you like to join me for a coffee at least, or a meal? My favourite is Eggs Benedict and the quality is to kill for." Linda accepted and they went along to the café together. Jon later admitted that may have been a poor choice of language, considering Linda's line of work, but then they went on to discuss other aspects of living in Spring Street including the quality of concierge staff and the ease of living there. Linda asked if he had ever eaten at Citta Restaurant, probably one of the top restaurants in Melbourne, and right on their doorstop; Jonathan could not resist asking with a smile, "why should I?" Linda had to admit she had once or twice and enjoyed the menu.

She volunteered that she seldom or never used the sporting facilities in the building because of the equipment available at police headquarters. The simple meal was over in 45 minutes with both of them having unobtrusively studied the other's body language.

Almost in passing, Linda was inquisitive enough to say, "What thing does a modern man like you enjoy doing?"

His considered reply was, "I enjoy a number of things, as and when the need arises!" Linda—with her trained police ear—picked up his different accent, but was astute enough not to enquire as to its origin as she could tell he was being evasive about his personal life. Jon had immediately picked up on Linda's South African accent but asked no questions. To Linda, this was a refreshing change to have no one prying into her life. Just taking things easily.

Maybe to illustrate his natural simplicity, he pointed out his enjoyment and appreciation of the view from their table in the corner of Café Excello looking across to Parliament House, at the gardens and statues, and more particularly the tranquillity. Chatting intermittently, they returned to the apartment block and went their separate ways with a casual, "let's get together again sometime."

In both cases, the first thing each did was to Google the other. For Jonathan, the most interesting thing was Linda's South African background. For Linda, the biggest interest was what or where Jonathan was before South Africa? Was that an American accent? When in doubt, or very curious—take the next small step!

Chapter 28

Intimacy

Coincidence or not, one Sunday morning Linda and Jon were both in their foyer, dressed in smart casual clothes, apparently after separate meetings held in the Lounge that came to a conclusion almost simultaneously. People broke off in different directions and Linda took the initiative by asking Jonathan, "Do you fancy a coffee across the park at KereKere Cafe?"

As he knew it well, he responded, "Sure do."

Off they strolled together across Lansdowne Street, past the Conservatory in the Fitzroy Gardens close to Cook's Cottage to the cafe. It probably was one of the most casual and relaxed meetings both had had for months, or even years. They talked about shared South African memories without constraints or placing any political blame. Neither had recommendations or solutions, mainly sadness for the lack of remedies for the country. Linda spoke with deep love and strong feelings for her family and childhood days there in a bygone era. Jon could or would only add highlights of his time in Cape Town, and some small details and often entertaining events as he had travelled the country widely. He offered no information about family or growing up, making only a comment or two of US and European ancestry and wide travels. He avoided any reference to Zimbabwe, Namibia, Mozambique etc or hunting concessions, or the 'people's revolutionary army' and its horrors; the things that can affect a person permanently. He seemed to be enjoying the warmth of the day and Linda's company at KereKere Café and he relaxed, and it rubbed off on them both, as they began to enjoy what appeared to be a growing relationship. Linda realised that Jon was genuinely shy but also extremely private. Occasional small physical touches sent warm impulses down one another's arms. Both showed relaxation as they shared some facets of their diverse and different backgrounds. No great horrors in Linda's recollections except some of the fear and physical violence that was a factor in her parents' decision to voluntarily leave South Africa and settle in Perth, Western Australia.

This meeting was not perceived by Linda or Jon then as the beginning of an in-depth sexual relationship. He, because of his secretive lifestyle—or more correctly his fugitive attitude—did not contemplate a relationship with anyone. She because her attitude was more like 'once bitten twice shy': Her previous long-term relationship with Jack which had been broken off after her fling in the US had created guilt and doubts about her capacity for loyalty. Both had slightly narcissistic personalities so were reluctant to overexpose any feelings too quickly in case they were not reciprocated. Be that as it may, they did recognise feelings of a slow-burning romance. Each realised they were no longer spring chickens though certainly not middle-aged. For Jonathan it was a time for retrospective consideration of his limited romances and sexual experiences. How well equipped was he to romance someone he cared for? He let that thought roll around in his mind for some time. He concluded that apart from his intense teenage romance with his second cousin Kathy in New York, his only other experience had been rough-and-tumble encounters with strangers or prostitutes. Sad really, but connected to the 'under the radar' lifestyle he had chosen as part of disappearing.

In spite of reservations and hesitations and the deliberate 'go slow,' an attitude of little things mean a lot gained momentum between them. Much of their chat, however, was kept superficial as they remained reticent to volunteer personal information about their backgrounds. Trust was growing slowly. They wandered comfortably back across the two beautiful parks in the sunshine and agreed to meet in the foyer in one week, at a time that was good for both of them. It was to be for a casual pizza around 7.30pm on a Tuesday as that fitted best Linda's tight dairy.

If nothing else, Jonathan considered himself to be 'a thinking man'. He reminded himself over and over that he owed nothing to anyone. Trust and promises were considered irrelevant, as he gave it all much deep thought. He was not seeking any redemption and felt an old saying, 'little is better', would suffice. He laughed when examining his own thoughts and said to himself, "I will duck and I will dive and I always survive!"

At the same time Linda was reviewing her own position. She was very busy with police work. Her career responsibilities were heavy within her job as leader of a section concentrating on international syndicates involving human slavery, drugs and tobacco, and money laundering—a diverse group of duties that required her to attend many meetings, conferences, leadership forums and morale-building events. Within the police force, trust and promise is mixed up with ambition and integrity. As she often said, "I'm glad I don't also have undercover divisions!" She tried not to be petty, not take sides, and to see the bigger picture. She knew she was blessed to be reporting directly to Superintendent Brunton, who was close and supportive. Because of her seniority and success, she was regularly recruited to give keynote addresses and motivational short presentations.

She considered one of the most meaningful quotes she had come across to be Dwight D. Eisenhower's, "You know, farming looks easy when your plough is a pencil, and you are a thousand miles from the cornfield!"

Chapter 29

Linda and Jon: Getting Together

The first person to note the new 'friendship' was the Concierge. As arranged, Linda and Jon met in the foyer with jackets and caps to stroll along Flinders Lane to Tario's in Duckworth Lane. It was a balmy evening despite a wicked breeze along the lane, and both evinced a languid demeanour to cover any nervousness. Once inside and out of the cold breeze, jackets were off and Linda let her fair hair fall loose down to her collar. Jon noted to himself he had not seen her so casual before. They each ordered a small pizza to be cut in half and shared. Both ordered a glass of shiraz and settled in to enjoy themselves in the ambience. The old-fashioned behaviour connected to early romance did not completely apply to the relationship, but also not for them, any 'straight to the business end' of sex. Nor the really old-fashioned pursuing, wooing, and any touch-by-touch restraints and patience. They were no longer teenagers.

The pizzas were as expected as was the second glass of house shiraz. Conversation rolled along without pause and more exploration continued. Jon noted how slim and slender Linda was, as he appreciated her not in her formal work clothing. He had noticed previously her athletic legs and small compact body, and a gold necklace she wore.

Jon was not aware that in turn Linda was appraising the smart casual clothes he was wearing, and how they emphasised his 6-foot 2 inch height, and how taut his body was. They were each silently congratulating themselves on their choice of partner. The food and service were excellent and they decided it was time to exit without coffee. Both could feel the sexual tension building. They gave each other warm smiles like genuine friends. Walking up Flinders Lane and crossing to the other side their hands briefly touched and fingers interlocked, sending fireworks through Linda's body.

Arriving in the foyer of the apartments Linda asked, "Come up for coffee?"

The answer with not too much emphasis from Jon, "Yes, please!" Jon was keen to see Linda's apartment. The 2Bed 2Baths were quite efficient in their layout and, as anticipated, the decor was similar to his unit and modern, and the apartment neat and tidy. The floor to ceiling windows made the unit very open and light, and blinds and drapes were comfortable but not necessary at all for privacy. Linda went to put coffee on and to shed a few things.

When she returned her hair clasp, light jacket and scarf had gone. "Coffee to go" she announced in a formal silly voice, as Jon shed his jacket and sprawled comfortably on the large leather couch.

He retorted, "Coffee in a blink" as they had some fun. They genuinely enjoyed together the stunning scenery, light orchestral music that had commenced from the large smart TV, and the city lights, the huge windows taking in large sections of Melbourne. In what seemed no time, they exchanged their first kiss on the lips. Then Jon kissed gently around her mouth ears, eyes and neck. Progress to undoing her blouse meant that he was able to caress her breasts and extract a warm sigh from Linda as her hands explored the belt, shirt, trousers worn by Jon. It was by mutual agreement and high sexual tension that they hobbled off to the main bedroom as more clothing was discarded, and the embracing became more urgent, accompanied by soft and warm expressions of enjoyment. There was excitement and an exhilarating sense of new beginnings for them both. They flopped onto the large bed together, almost naked. Warmth and energy flowed through veins as more and more they explored. Jon was exploring her neck and quickly moved down to gently first one then the other nipple. Finger and tongue arrived at the target simultaneously. Linda murmured sweet nothings as her whole body began to arch. It seemed before she knew it, Jonathan had entered her and she uttered a small exclamation of satisfaction.

Permission given and willingly received. With gentleness and slowness, and remembering experiences from afar or history, they set about pleasuring one another. They rode together gently and sensually with rhythm of hips to a gasping climax together. The missionary position was natural but with huge enthusiasm and some physical dexterity Linda found herself with legs wrapped around Jon's waist and arriving at her second climax with head arched back without a problem. The words delightful and delicious ran through her brain. They lay together entangled for many long minutes afterwards and both drifted off.

Perhaps an hour or two later Linda asked teasingly, "How come you are such an expert on how to please a girl?"

Slightly tongue in cheek, Jon's answer was, "I have read a lot of books and seen a lot of movies!" He thought at this stage, it correct to agree, as they hardly knew each other. They were enjoying the moments!

Later they could not remember who asked the obvious, "Was this a one-off, how long have we known each other?" Reality began to set in; the questions flowed, "How well do we really know each other? Will we see each other again? What will be the outcome?" Both admitted the urgent wish to do it all over again.

Rattling around in Jonathan's head as he continued what was probably the most enjoyable moment in his adult life was the song by Peter Sarstedt, 'Where do you go to (my Lovely)'? He was almost afraid to ask Linda if she knew the song. But he did and her response was. "Oh yes! I love it!" Many of the lines reverberated, some in different ways, for each of them but surprisingly in similar ways by interpretation. It seemed a little lighthearted to examine the lyrics just for fun to check it out, but they both agreed it was worthwhile to give it a go. They tried to select lyrics that could pertain to themselves and with some poetic licence apply to 'others' they knew. They were still wrapped in the warmth of their embraces as they googled the song and went through the lines:

"But where do you go to, my lovely
When you're alone in your bed?
Tell me the thoughts that surround you
I want to look inside your head, yes, I do

But where do you go to, my lovely
When you're alone in your bed?
Won't you tell me the thoughts that surround you?
I want to look inside your head, yes, I do

You talk like Marlene Dietrich
And you dance like Zizi Jeanmaire
Your clothes are all made by Balmain
And there's diamonds and pearls in your hair, yes, there are

You live in a fancy apartment
Off the Boulevard St. Michel
Where you keep your Rolling Stones records
And a friend of Sacha Distel, yes, you do

Your name it is heard in high places
You know the Aga Khan
He sent you a race horse for Christmas
And you keep it just for fun, for a laugh, ha-ha-ha

They say that when you get married
It'll be to a millionaire
But they don't realize where you came from,
and I wonder if they really care, or give a damn

I remember the back streets of Naples
Two children begging in rags
Both touched with a burning ambition
To shake off their lowly-born tags, they tried

So, look into my face, Marie-Claire
And remember just who you are
Then go and forget me forever
But I know you still bear the scar, deep inside, yes, you do

I know where you go to, my lovely
When you're alone in your bed
I know the thoughts that surround
Cause I can look inside your head."

There was at least another verse about qualifications, sipping Napoleon Brandy without getting lips wet, and stealing a Picasso painting. A wonderful mixture of inquisition and humour, giving Jon and Linda chances to sing along and examine their own backgrounds. They both wondered if it was helping in the 'getting to know you' process. It seemed like it could be the theme for a future together. Both of them expressed the view, "The best is yet to come."

Chapter 30

Superintendent Ron Brunton

For Linda Alexander, her responsibilities were ever increasing, as unfortunately her direct boss, Superintendent Ron Brunton, with whom she had enjoyed an excellent long-term relationship, announced his earlier than expected retirement due to sudden ill health. This meant a series of changes and new internal relationships that inevitably involved Linda.

The personal ramifications were huge as Ron has been her champion, mentor, friend, and supported her throughout her career. Most of all she grieved for her friend's terminal prognosis. Brunton's illness rattled Linda's composure as the police force for many years had been her protective life bubble. It was all she knew, and he had always been in it. Internally, she had really only had Brunton and Beth, the latter to whom she was able to vent, in times of stress. Growing status and seniority had its downsides. Criminality was getting more sophisticated in Australia as elsewhere, with greater reliance on IT. Linda was very expert but remote from the more basic lifestyles of average people. Her growing intimate relationship with Jon Smithson was by now a good prop for her.

Ron Brunton urged her to apply for a promotion to his position.

Chapter 31

Bounty Hunter 14 Has Not Given Up

Searcher 14 returned home to New York from Melbourne and referred to the Codona solicitor in New York, seeking clarification of many points and elaboration on others. He was given the name and address of the senior family member who still retained enthusiasm for the search. Having been assured the bounty still existed, he made an appointment to meet in New York to seek further details from older brother Credi Codona, now the head of the family. Years had passed and patriarch Patrin Codona had died, but family anger had not dissipated. Credi confirmed the bounty, and as it was in a trust earning interest, the value had reached in excess of US$100,000.

Credi willingly volunteered personal details. Hanzi aka Hans, would now be middle aged, with brown eyes and probably dark hair greying around the temples, around 170cm high, and swarthy. Perhaps unlikely to have tattoos, unless for disguise. He had a good singing voice. Hanzi also had had excellent circus skills, and was still probably physically fit.

Searcher 14 had heard about Aron Brodsky whilst in Melbourne, but Credi thought Australia an unlikely place for Hans. His opinion was he was more likely in Italy, Romania or Poland or even further east. Searcher 14 had time and finance on his side, and restarted the Codona search armed now with greater detail, and a photo of the target when a young man. He thought employment in a circus unlikely.

Chapter 32

Becoming More Intimately Acquainted
Linda's past cases

As their comfort with each other grew, Linda and Jon decided to be open with each other, with an unspoken agreement on confidentiality as they chatted on as occasions allowed, with Linda often taking the lead. Ringing in her ears was a caution from Beth Jenkins not to ignore her entrenched, but seldom said out loud, VicPol nickname of 'Lonely Linda'. So, she decided to relax a bit and enjoy Jon's company, and as she added to herself, "I like him!" The fact was that their feelings were deepening into love and they wanted each other physically all the time. It helped immensely that they really did like each other as well. They also realised that desire is not a privilege only enjoyed or limited to youth.

Linda was growing more comfortable with Jon each and every day. Through relaxing weekends together in Malmsbury in the Macedon Ranges, or in Melbourne CBD, they were getting to know each other more profoundly.

However, policework by its very nature could be a lonely place, and so many jobs were by delegation. The really serious criminals came in many guises, from the international crime syndicates, vicious family and gang turf wars and paybacks, through to daylight shootings. Add tobacco and drugs to old-fashioned burglaries-to-order. It was complex and serious work. The possibility of further promotion added fuel to her fire and yet she felt some hesitation, a small chink in her overall confidence. The police culture was mature but did not preclude petty jealousies and 'one upmanship' often enough.

Linda told Jon about her general sexual history; from a first experience way back in South Africa at 18 years of age through to a not so genuine affair with a married police associate in Perth where she was left dangling, and a more comfortable longer relationship with a genuine friend and lover, Jeremy. She lightly touched on her recent partner Jack and that she was now single, without going into much detail.

She also spoke to Jon, over time, about highlights of her police career in Victoria. Cases that included a complicated arson-murder in the shopping precinct of Ballarat, with family interests involved in various directions. Linda had been joined by Beth Jenkins then, and also on her next case in Woodend in the Macedon Ranges, involving the twin Moretti brothers, which took some extraordinary twists including murder and mutilation.

She also told him about her most recent major case triumph in which she had been involved with two other very different women. The first woman was a troubled narcissist; highly intelligent and ambitious, a school teacher who wanted to follow in Linda's footsteps as a police officer. The second woman was a clever international prostitute involved in money laundering and human trafficking, with drugs and high-profile local people involved. The culmination of that case was a spectacular drug bust and shootout at midnight in which a female criminal was killed and Linda was shot and wounded in the shoulder. A short stay in hospital followed but she was back at work within days!

It was a serious learning curve for Jonathan, and he told her, "I want to know more." However, he also knew he could not ever hope to match her stories, or share such personal information with her.

They both enjoyed food and wine, and the opportunity for time-out in a loving atmosphere. In little snippets and over time, Jon did attempt to volunteer some of his past. He in turn asked her for trust and confidentiality. His first attempt at trying to establish his sensitivity was to say in general, "How can the human race build things of great beauty, such as artworks, buildings, poetry, love stories, monuments over long periods of history, and then in a short burst, set about destroying it all? There is something seriously astray in modern psychology and all the complications created by evil in history." Still exercising great care and caution, he decided that it was time to ease up a little on his fanaticism over personal security. He realised the dangers of the deeper feelings growing for Linda but his wish was to earn her respect by his disclosures.

Deciding how far back to go presented a huge dilemma for him. And when to tell her. With genuine care, he decided it would be over a meal at what was now one of their favourite eating spots, the European Restaurant at 161 Spring Street, just a short stroll along from their apartments. The European was one of the oldest established restaurants in Melbourne and a timeless place. Decorated with mirrored walls, wood panels, old posters, it had often been used in the past for shots of old European cities. Jon thought it in particular a really good spot for some disclosures. He was not sure whether he would get into describing any European cities but perhaps they could adjourn to the Wine Shop or the Supper Club afterwards.

Stressing that he had no criminal record anywhere, nor was he on an Interpol search list, or on any internal lists held by police in any country, he launched into his story of how he had joined the French Foreign Legion by knocking on the door of a recruiting centre in Paris. The basic requirement was to be single and to sign up for five years, providing you passed the three-week selection process.

This process had been rigorous and he volunteered that although the Foreign Legion required no ID, his ID then had been false. Once an accepted Legionnaire, he told Linda he had really loved being a member and all it stood for. The pay was ordinary but increased depending on rank and length of service in the Legion. He had quickly learnt to speak fluent French and to understand the meaning of loyalty. Jon told Linda he was promoted and learnt about the culture of honour in the world-famous Legion. He matured without realising it, became hardened in many ways and joined in group celebrations to honour events. The Foreign Legion had become his whole life and provided him with everything he needed at the time. Free accommodation, free food, free clothing. Plus a huge range of skills including how to survive. Jon said he left after four years with full FFL approval, and the chance to create a new person with a new name. He told her he had saved a significant amount of money, and made a wide range of contacts in Africa.

Linda was well aware of the difficulty Jon was having in elaborating on his personal life but by nature and training she was an excellent listener who did not interrupt his flow even when her curiosity was almost begging for more. She withheld her questions.

In a much vaguer way, Jon described wandering through several southern African countries working in various jobs before moving on. Some jobs, where the maxim 'no names, no pack drill' was applied, were lucrative and well rewarded. Survival was the main factor.

The first country in which he had needed to establish a real identity, he told Linda, was in Southern Rhodesia/Zimbabwe. There was turmoil there after 1965 when Ian Smith unilaterally declared an independent country. Financially, it had been a well organised commercial entity for a minority of people. There were many shonky activities. Jon admitted he became expert in trading only in cash and not hesitating to use unusual methods to expedite results. Keeping on the move, he remembered a saying his father had used, "moss does not grow on rolling stones". Zimbabwe presented the opportunity for independent companies and traders to take advantage, even though the country itself was rushing downhill as many of the older and skilled businesses and were leaving like 'rats deserting a sinking ship'.

This in broad terms could be seen similarly to how Linda's family much later viewed the South African situation. Jonathan realised he was climbing close to her parallel.

As the evening progressed, and they moved into the Wine Shop and Supper Club, Linda, wanting to show her emotional support, literally exploded into Jonathan's embrace. For a moment or two, they forgot their reticence to show emotion in public.

Linda tried to help by asking about his Harley Davidson, but Jon dismissed that as more a midlife crisis than a link to some of the nefarious connections he had in Southern Africa. He wanted to explain more about the lawlessness that existed in numerous ways there, and began by explaining how the Zimbabwe, Mozambique and South African borders come together at the junction through the Kruger Park. Linda of course would know of the park—an enormous government game park created for the people of South Africa to enjoy wild animal viewing.

In Mozambique in particular—with its Portuguese historical background and large range of Bantu tribes and dialects, the official language still Portuguese and English only spoken in hotels and lodges—poaching was rampant. Illegal trading, particularly in elephant tusks, was violent and lawless. Poachers roamed widely, heavily armed, and had no respect for the law. Linda knew not much of the detail.

Jon was relaxed and waxed lyrical as he described the openness of the game park. Linda had been often with her parents and as the evening wore on and names like Limpopo, Phalaborwa, Letaba, Oliphants, Satara, Skukuza, Lower Sabie, and Pretoriuskop rolled off their tongues they became more and more animated. The Rondavels accommodation, and the exit from the park through Malelane and then Nelspruit seemed like an anti-climax to their wonderful evening.

Jon admitted to Linda that in his own mind he viewed himself as a man on the run. He knew he was not in any formal witness protection program, as for someone accused of a major misdemeanour. But he had run through many countries trying to hide his real self and as time passed, normal communications had become more intrusive. "Man on the run" was his own label. Although he did not say so to Linda, he of course knew why he had given himself that label—there was likely at any time to be a new 'hunter'. There might not be anything so dramatic as a witness code number in some international police database attached to him, but Jon knew he had to be constantly ultra careful.

Their level of comfort with each other had deepened greatly as they wandered happily back along Spring Street past the Old Treasury Building to home. No temptation at that time of night to enjoy a stroll in the park. Jon hadn't ventured far back into his history even though he was keen to be more open and to create more evidence for trust. In a small concession to privacy, he volunteered an old family saying he credited to his father, "It's never wrong to do the right thing." He alluded to fun and games he had played with his siblings in what he recalled as his trouble-free times of youth. By being ultra careful, he also realised that Linda—or any woman he wished to be permanently engaged with—would require more than just a passing flirtation, no matter how pleasant that may be. Particularly when he was clearly in his early forties.

He modestly admitted he had been able to arrive in Australia with adequate funds. To lighten the discussion on how money and valuables had been smuggled in from Southern Africa, Jon delved into two of the known methods that he would not claim as his own but alluded to as possible. One was diamonds secreted in his own walking stick and secondly, South Africa had an unusual law that modern cars had to have retro fitted large front and back bumpers that could safely absorb collisions with minimal damage to vehicle or persons. Great hiding spots, he said!

These small insights shared made them both look at one another often with new eyes. Jon knew he was seeing Linda through rose-tinted glasses whenever they met socially and she was not dressed or behaving as a police officer. He thought Linda quite petite, and a fine-tuned athlete with a very smart analytical brain.

Linda in turn saw Jon as a middle-aged well-groomed 'new Australian', an American of European extraction. Nicely tanned, with mid-length brown hair, greying at the temples, tall, with a well-proportioned body and legs that could have belonged to a rugby player.

Chapter 33

Superintendent Brunton: Replacement

Internally the police team culture was beginning to crack around the edges as more members began to express interest in the appointment to replace Superintendent Ron Brunton. Petty jealousies began to surface and various members began to put pressure on Linda, either in support with encouragement, or in false sympathy about a new boss. Linda spent time with Beth, her closest friend and ally.

Human nature came to the fore as rivalries and selection criteria were outlined. It did seem that Linda was the likely choice but all proper steps had to be advertised and followed transparently. As in any competitive corporation, the knives were out and unknown sources were drawing from historical background 'facts' from Linda's past, even back to Perth. It was all very stressful for Linda. In many ways it accelerated her relationship with Jonathan and intensified the support she drew from him and from Beth Jenkins.

She and Jon were now spending a lot of time together, and the closeness and exchanges of innermost feelings regularly bubbled to the surface in intimate moments, and had Linda commenting on the idea of taking Jon to Perth to meet her parents. It was suggested in the mildest possible way without any time association or reciprocal move from Jon. While a total no-response reaction from him, it made him think for the first time for years and years about his family, and he wondered to himself about their welfare and location, still in the US. He thought about his heritage from Romania; were they from Bucharest, Bulgaria, Poland, or even the five percent of Hungarians speaking Romanian in Romania? Wonder... wonder... where are they from?

Linda decided a trip to Perth would be timely, and went ahead and booked a week mainly at Rottnest Island for them, with two free days to meet with her parents, John and Prue Alexander, who were now long-established permanent residents in Perth. They were delighted to know Linda was coming and to have the opportunity to meet her new companion, of whom they knew little.

After arriving at Rottnest Island, just 30 minutes by ferry from Perth, Jon thought it quite remarkable. An ideal island on which there were many ways to relax and recharge. The Australian native quokka is both a rare and friendly inhabitant when seen. Accommodation varied from camping sites to the Samphire Rottnest Hotel where Linda had booked them in.

There were plenty of tours for them to consider and time just to sit around relaxing, enjoying the beaches and being together.

It was a great opportunity to use more time exploring one another physically and mentally. The feelings of mutual trust between them grew with each confidence exchanged. Linda was learning that Jon had a quirky sense of humour which did not always bubble to the surface but he had a saying that he occasionally used to her, "Curiosity killed the cat!" She was recognising how swiftly his brain worked and how he was a 'skimmer over' of facts. Or was it being an 'avoider'?

They talked a lot about her boss Super Ron Brunton, how sad she was about his declining health and whether she had the right qualifications, skills and maturity to go for the more senior job.

However, for Jonathan, to be meeting her parents indicated a new level of intimacy that held serious ramifications. Deep waters! Linda had already anticipated there would be questions from her parents and friends about his age and background, and she and Jonathan did chat about that beforehand.

John and Prue Alexander were indeed happy but also curious to host Linda and her new love. Their curiosity went deeper than casual as they had come from a long family history in Southern Africa and had been told very little about Jonathan Smithson and his background. So, plenty in the immediate to talk about. The word 'suspicious' rattled around in their minds, as they tried not to ask too many probing questions about his family or personal journey.

Chapter 34

Hunter 14

Hunter 14—now known to be named Neville McPherson—became a much more intense chaser of the bounty reward. He was formidable, as a private citizen best described as being 'of private means'. He was a US citizen from a middle-class background, university educated, single and unencumbered, and someone known to be successful in his endeavours. He had heard about the past 'upset' amongst a well-known circus family, the angst caused, and the bounty offered. Some of this was now like a legend.

He had decided it was worthwhile to dig deeper.

Everyone needs a little luck in life and in the early stage of his endeavours, Neville McPherson had a couple of sheer flukes. He spent no time in Europe or Africa but assumed there was a connection in Australia through the murder of Brodsky, details of which were given to him by connections in New York City, and he headed off to start his new search, this time in Sydney. After finding accommodation at an ordinary hotel in Kings Cross, he did the rounds of police and what circuses he could find but came up with virtually nothing. A few in the Kings Cross area vaguely remembered an American spending money on enquiries as to the same subject. He was interested in any leads but most suggested that Brodsky went down to Melbourne and that was where he was murdered. No connection whatever to circuses in Sydney.

McPherson decided to return to Melbourne, moving into accommodation near the Southern Cross Station, at the western end of Bourke Street—close to Vic Police headquarters, and went about his search in a low-key fashion. His research had by now told him that Hans Codona was about six feet tall, with brown hair, a dark complexion and athletic build. No doubt living under a new name. He probably had lost most of his American accent, and spoke Australian English with maybe a European clip, even French. Maybe by now he had moved on from his working class beginnings, had perhaps earned a uni degree and used it in his work—one of the suit and tie brigade? With his background, he was probably not at all frightened to use violence to protect his confidentiality.

While in Sydney, McPherson had been told of the headless clown murder in Melbourne, and he had been recommended to visit the police station in East Melbourne. He now did so, and was informed the case had been solved with the arrest and trial of two bikies; he was referred on to DSS Beth Jenkins who was helpful but offered no further information other than court proceedings had been finalised. There was no help from her on who the clown may have been.

McPherson was unhappy with this information and kept his enquiries going. He relayed his frustrations back to the elderly lawyer in New York who was the nominated family contact, but received no additional help there. In fact it set off 'tip-offs' to Jon's listening post in Chicago, who sent a long communication back to Jonathan. It was agreed that the nuisance value of this very old family matter should be concluded and some form of mild enquiry to the family should be pursued.

In the meantime, Jon decided a 'dissuader' should be given to McPherson, serious enough, with compensation, to assure he would never be involved again. This required extreme care and confidentiality. Everything at full arm's length and in great detail. The McPherson matter was to be handled first. This was to be arranged from overseas using the same crime syndicate contacts previously used. He was to be captured in the rental car he was using, taken to a remote site and given a mild physical beating and acquainted with a bit of folklore known as, 'Molly Whuppie', the essence of which was, "Fee Fi Fo Fum, 'Woe betide ye Molly Whuppie, if you ever come here again!" All a bit of Jonathan humour. The seriousness of intent, however, was not to be undervalued. The message for McPherson was to be strengthened after the beating by taking him in the car which was then to be set alight. He was to be rescued only at the last minute, given medical treatment for any physical damage done and put on a flight directly back to the US. This Jonathan had to arrange through his US agent.

The message was to be given loud and clear that no more details were to be given out to any new 'would be' bounty hunters. Jon also instructed his agent to arrange an anonymous approach to be made to the Codona family to investigate the worth of any possible communications about concluding the search? And any payment of rewards or compensation required to them.

Contact was made with Daniel Cohen, of Elsner and Sommer Lawyers, to pass on this olive branch to the Codona family in New York. That stirred up old emotions, and giving up the hunt was not considered. In fact it renewed energy into finding the wayward son. On his return to the US, McPherson, in spite of the assault—and because of it—was now totally convinced of the likelihood that Hans Codona was residing in Australia.

Chapter 35

Alexander Family in Perth

With agreement from Jonathan, Linda booked air fares and accommodation for another week, now staying at the Adnate Hotel, which was in Perth and described as part of an 'Art Series' with a five-star rating and small enough to be considered boutique. It was a short distance from where her parents lived in Cottesloe and close enough for casual lunches with old friends and family.

The first evening in Perth her parents put on a semi-casual supper of salads, cold meats, fruit and ice cream and a glass of Stellenbosch wine as a casual welcome to their home, with the intent of a relaxed 'getting to know you' evening. Naturally enough conversation began with frequent hesitations, as John and Prue looked for common ground. The wine from Stellenbosch was appreciated and mention of the family living in Johannesburg was an opportunity to talk about 'places been'. Jon was not forthcoming in that area but still open and friendly.

John Anderson was more forthright, saying, "Linda has told us you did time with the French Foreign Legion?"

A little surprised, Jon responded, "Correct, but that was a long time ago." No putdown was intended or taken.

Prue, being ever helpful, asked, "Have you ever been to Namibia,

Jonathan, which was formerly known as South West Africa?"

Jon responded enthusiastically, "Yes, I have, it's one of the most sparsely populated countries in the world, and has the driest, most stunning countryside. I did business there, mostly in Windhoek."

Probably as anticipated, Linda's father lightly asked what type of business. Jon was relaxed and his response was to emphasise all the boundaries Namibia had, of the Atlantic Ocean, South Africa, Angola, Botswana, and a long narrow tract that led to Zambia and Zimbabwe. He added, "I know you will be aware of that, but that alone makes it most interesting!" He expanded in general terms on all the mining activities there and diamond trading.

Jon then looked over to John and Prue and asked, "Have you ever been to the Etosha Pan or Lake Otjikoto in Namibia?" A no from Prue, and a partial yes from John. That got a laugh. Jon was vaguely aware of Linda's parents' history of education and achievements in South Africa and their quick appointments to senior positions in Perth. It would follow that they were conservative in a political sense. Prue worked for BHP and John, as a senior hospital medical officer, was on the cusp of setting up his own consultancy. They were a successful pair in Perth.

Linda was enjoying the evening and the conversation. Jon kept things very much at a general level, and his next question lowered any possible intensity, by asking Prue in particular what her favourite spots in South Africa were, to which she replied without much hesitation, Cape Town, Swaziland, and the game parks, with Kruger Park in particular for the many holidays enjoyed there with the family.

General conversation flowed over chocolates and coffee, until John asked if Jon had ever been to Gaborone. "Oh yes, I know it well," he replied. An inquisitive look appeared on the three faces of those listening, and Jon followed up with, "The capital of Botswana, where there is a great game reserve and the famous 'Three Dikgosi Monument'."

Trying to deflect any more speculation about his past, Jon suggested it might be the subject for another time as Botswana, along with Zambia, Angola and Zimbabwe, were all countries he had done business in; silence for a moment or two until a more general light-hearted conversation resumed and continued through to 'home time'.

They all agreed to meet again for lunch tomorrow as Prue and John had taken days off to suit. Once back in their hotel room, Linda was quick to inform Jon with genuine thanks that she had learned a lot more about him than he had previously spoken about.

His reply with a short laugh was, "you all deserve to know me better!"

Next day at a beautiful café on the water's edge in Fremantle, exchanges continued in a laidback and friendly style. A glass of local reisling to accompany the first of a mostly fish meal enabled the relaxed talks to begin again amongst the family members and Jon.

As John had promised at home to Prue, he asked a direct question of Jon, "Is home for you Australia, and in particular your address in Melbourne?"

Jon gave a warm smile and laughed as he answered, "Now that's a good direct question that deserves a slightly wider answer. Yes, my official address is in Spring Street—and for my various commercial interests I have that address and for my driver's licence. I do have interests in other properties, and during my short stay in Perth I have joined the Eagles AFL club!" That got a good laugh.

In an effort to generalise the conversation again, Jon asked if the family had fond memories of places in South Africa such as Nelspruit and Kruger Park, which he said were still favourites of his. He added another question, "Did you and the family ever visit Bophuthatswana and enjoy any of the fantastic shows at Sun City?" This caused a mixed reaction from Prue and John as they appeared reluctant to describe its history and eventual absorption and naming, into the Orange Free State and later Free State Province. A much warmer reaction was achieved with an emphasis on the awe-inspiring beauty of the Victoria Falls in Zimbabwe, with its 108-metre height. Prue and Linda both went into raptures about the unique size and grandeur of the mighty Falls, which drop from the Zambezi River. John asked the next question, "Jon, I imagine with your wide experience you know Harare in Zimbabwe well?"

Jon's response was calm and friendly, "Yes, I even learned to speak adequate basic Bantu to mix freely with the ninety-eight percent who used the language. A fun fact; there are sixteen official languages there — the most in the world! Yes, I did business there. Harare is now a long way from the old Salisbury," he said.

John and Prue both added how troubled Zimbabwe had been and still how lawless in many ways. Jon could hardly suppress a smile.

Lunch went on harmoniously as plans for some local WA tourism were made and an arrangement for another get-together in two days' time. Jonathan was aware of the gentle cross-examination he was being given, and it set off in his own mind again whether maybe it was time for some investigating of his own about his family in New York or even Romania, or wherever they may now be domiciled. Inbuilt caution warned him of the potential dangers, even if he had trust in the security and anonymity of his new persona. It did emphasise for him how deeply he was starting to feel for Linda and how his personal life could be restricted. For the first time ever, he could see a future with another.

While on holiday at the lovely Adnate Hotel Perth, with the warm family attention, the relaxed evenings had an effect on them both and they enjoyed more intense love making.

All the events and sharing of intimacies came crashing to a halt when Linda received a telephone call from Sergeant Beth Jenkins, followed by a regulation email informing her of the sudden death of Ron Brunton. All personal plans were suspended, as Linda arranged to fly back to Melbourne. Jonathan had no doubt succeeded in convincing the family he was a person of substance.

On her return, Linda was invited into a meeting with senior personnel asking her to make herself a candidate for the replacement of Superintendent Brunton. Part of the discussion was to advise her of the different roles and responsibilities the position would cover. Those were yet to be finally decided, but they wanted to indicate that her interest would be welcomed. Good news for Linda. She reminded herself, "Take a deep breath; it calms the mind!"

Chapter 36

Ron Brunton: Death

With great sadness, it was officially announced within the police force that Superintendent Brunton had died. Condolences were passed on to family, friends and police associates with the advice that full funeral details were to follow. A statement was issued that a temporary appointment had been made to cover his responsibilities while a search for his permanent replacement was made. It was brief and to the point.

The wheels began to turn and candidates considered their chances. Linda was truly distressed by Ron's passing and had huge problems getting her thoughts together to commence becoming an applicant. Along with all the activity around funeral arrangements, Linda perceived the need for a 'fresh' discussion on police culture to remind her of some of the difficulties her application would pose. Not least was the 'Old Boys Club' which did not even acknowledge that prejudices still existed. To aid in the mental preparation for herself and even for Beth Jenkins, the pair agreed to have several one-hour coffee meetings offsite to push on with getting themselves up to speed.

They chatted about the fast pace of change; about Vic Pol careers, detective qualifications, additional education, human resources, career paths, information technology, and wondered about DNA and the role of AI in their future roles. Specialist positions such as forensic scientists, data analysts and fingerprint experts seemed to be coming more specialised by the day! Financial and legal crime was becoming far more sophisticated. Linda in particular wanted to theorise about things that could be enacted under a change of regime, if she succeeded in being appointed Superintendent. This was no shallow contemplation as she was full of doubts as to whether she had the 'bottle' for the job. The more she researched, the bigger the task seemed to become. A timely glass of red wine was a good soother and relaxer. Like most optimistic and positive people, they both agreed there would be chances to grow into the role.

The appointment would be made by the Chief Superintendent, who no doubt would have all the time and documentation necessary to make an unbiased appointment on merit. It was stressful for all concerned.

A confidential word had been sent to Linda advising that the position (for PR reasons) would be advertised both internally and externally. The short list internally was of four well-qualified candidates who would be interviewed shortly, and who were encouraged to consider the reasons why they were well suited for the position and to be ready to comment confidentially to a panel.

Ron Brunton's funeral was very big and supported by a full turnout of all available police in full regalia, and was well covered by the media. Linda was in attendance, and the image of a unified police force was well and truly on display. However, internally rumours abounded, and as the steps involved in the appointment process were got underway, it all added more stress into Linda's life.

Her relationship with Jonathan was now well past being just a casual friendship. Disclosing confidential personal information back and forth added to their feelings of deep appreciation of each other.

And it was all accompanied by more wonderful physical sexual explorations and fulfilment. They had become one another's greatest confidantes. Confidentialities were gradually released amongst grand visions of mutual thoughtfulness, and the ultimate vision of concealing nothing. It was understood that Linda had much less deep and meaningful information to release.

This was the catalyst for Jon to plan a serious exploration of his family in various geographical areas. A big trip to Europe. A huge decision in itself, as it would need him to declare to Linda information known to him alone, some of it with criminal attachments.

Chapter 37

Jonathan Considers His Future

The two weeks spent in Perth enjoying the warmth of Linda and her family had highlighted for Jon the importance of family support and love, and reminded him sharply that he had no such relationships. For obvious reasons of course, but in his mind he considered what could or should he do?

He was well aware Linda needed no distractions at this point and she and her parents still had hundreds of unasked and unanswered questions in their minds. The words of a new song he had heard kept bubbling to the top of his brain, "Your embrace, some kind of wonderful...!" helped him realise how far down a new road he had evolved with Linda.

He came to a huge decision. He would go to Romania, beginning in Bucharest as a tourist and, extremely cautiously, enquire as to any extended family. He promised himself he would do deep research from Australia before venturing forth.

Discretion and confidentiality were the big necessities that screamed to him when embarking on such a venture.

Jon's first careful steps included visits to two very popular in-depth book shops; Dymocks in Collins Street and Hill of Content in Bourke Street, to purchase books on the history of Romania. He realised that with his grandparents having left Romania when they were young, his knowledge was quite sketchy, coming only from what they and his parents had told him in his youth.

He needed information on how to refresh (as a new Australian) his documents and what he had to do regarding passport, visas, health requirements etc. Were there any potential problems?

A visit to a large travel agency in Collins Street, almost next to Dymocks, for a casual general discussion with the first available sales assistant got enquiries underway, without his feeling any threat of disclosing any important details. It highlighted to him that it was nearly two decades since he had fled Europe as a desperado on the run but at the same time just a shame-faced kid.

There now exists in the EU an area called the Schengen Area that originated in 1985 and covered the countries of France, Germany, Belgium, Luxemburg and the Netherlands. It gradually expanded to become one of the largest free trade areas in the world. Bulgaria and Romania for their own reasons were reticent joiners. Most European countries required tourists to hold legitimate passports and 90-day visas.

It became apparent to Jonathan he would need to travel with care if he wanted to carry out much investigative action, at the risk of attracting some official notice. Initial low key research about the whereabouts of Gypsies, now generally termed Roma people, in Romania drew complete blanks. He thought he could remember some of the words from his grandparents and had stories of the Carpathian Mountains and well-preserved towns, churches and castles. He did remember being told that the family circus was able to move freely in and out of neighbouring countries.

What were known as 'Gypsies and Travellers' in the past are difficult to define because they are not a single homogenous group, but cover a range of groups with different histories, cultures and beliefs, commonly called Roma. He read with interest that there were

Romany Gypsies, Welsh Gypsies, Scottish Gypsies and Travellers and Irish Travellers. Romania had had the most of these peoples. They were nomads who migrated over the centuries throughout eastern Europe and gained a reputation as musicians, metalworkers traders, and thieves. In very general ways, they are mainly Christian.

This amount of detail for Jonathan was intriguing and fascinating. Most of it was absolutely 'new news'. Plucked out of references at random was a note that Roma girls and boys entered marriage before the age of eighteen and first cousins could marry.

Jon knew he was of Romanian heritage. He decided to enter Europe via France, specifically via the city of Strasbourg. He would wander his way east across to Romania to the capital city of Bucharest, a beautiful old city on the south-eastern shores of the Black Sea with a population of around 1½ million residents.

He had virtually nil memories of the city from two decades ago, when he was escaping from America, as he had been driven then by terror to escape as far away and as quickly as possible. He had spent little time in the city of Constanta, with no time to appreciate the Roman mosaics, Casino, or fourth-century tiles. He had almost the same lack of memories about Bucharest, with its wonderful Bucharest Metropolitan Circus, its Circus Globose, and the enormous famous permanent Big Top. He knew or had read about Dracula Castle and Transylvania, the famous brown bears, the Danube Delta, Carpathian Mountains, and the beauty of the towns and cities. There were many circuses. Most of the large towns or cities had resident or regular visiting circuses.

As Jonathan began to apply himself to the logistics involved, his mind wandered sometimes to Cousin Kathy and her second-cousin husband Alessandro Codona, as mature people. Where did they live? What was their lifestyle like?

Chapter 38

Jonathan Goes to Europe
In search of heritage

Jon announced to Linda, and to anyone else who needed to know, "He was going to Europe for personal reasons." He had carefully spoken with Linda first, telling her that he was going to address his personal background so he could share openly his history with her. He used the word 'pragmatic' to widen what he considered the merits of his trip. He emphasised that he was going to be sensible and realistic rather than over-theoretical to his considerations and research. He said he intended to apply business ethics.

He phoned a friend who was a psychologist and invited him out for coffee. He wanted to share that he understood how his personal experiences had shaped who he was—and that it wasn't just what he said, but how he said it, that also mattered. The friend asked him the following: Could he think on his feet? Did he ruffle easily? Was he persuasive? Could he think a lie and speak the truth? Or could he tell a lie, while he thought the truth?" Jon considered he could handle these types of confrontations well enough, and his friend gave the opinion he was adequately prepared for the trip, given the basics of the situation that Jonathan had given him. He had to ask himself, "What have I become?"

The next decisions were where to start, how to get there, and what help was needed. A bare necessity at each location had to be English-speaking local guides who could be trusted with confidentiality. He was aware of the need for extreme privacy even though his current Australian surname would not set off any alarms. He was aware that human nature often presented opportunities for exploitation and he would need to watch for that.

He had done research on recent history of the Codona family and was very interested in finding out more.

After discussions with a travel agent, he decided that the French city of Strasbourg would be his initial port of entry because of its size and international mix. Air fares through Singapore Airlines seemed easy and experienced guides would be available to check in where circuses may be active. Part of the plan was to be judged, by anyone who could be watching, as a completely lackadaisical rich tourist.

Jonathan Smithson would be difficult to classify by the ordinary observer. Slightly swarthy in appearance, travelling on an Australian passport but no obvious Aussie accent. His accent could be British or Irish; very international. No other passports or credit cards other than those issued in Sydney. Wearing cap and sunglasses he was indistinguishable from millions of other tourists wandering the streets of Europe.

His enquiries were to be mainly about circus performances rather than owners or star performers—all to find out more about the Codona family.

After arriving in Strasbourg, which seemed a very neutral place to organise his trip east, he experimented with his modus operandi. Visits to shows, and discreet telephone calls to owner operators, never mentioning the name Codona. With the aid of a local tourist guide supplied by his hotel, Jonathan did the sightseeing thing and made a visit to an afternoon showing at a major circus. He found it intriguing to be there, refreshing old memories of France.

Jon was amazed at the sheer quality of the international circus artists, the colourful backgrounds creating fantasies, the sound and volume of music, the spectacular sequences by trapeze and acrobats doing gravity-defying twists and turns, and the ground-based group of physical contortionists who made everyone gasp. It was like a visit to Fantasia.

For him, it was all a reminder of the skill and ability that used to run within his family. Reflections popped into his head, and he experienced a strange and recurring set of nightly dreams involving his cousin Katarina (Kathy) sitting opposite him at a campsite as he looked deeply into her eyes, repeating her name over and over, each time placing the emphasis on a different syllable to create a different-sounding name. How strange! He wondered what might have eventuated with Kathy had circumstances been different, and what had happened to the unborn child Jon had left her with? Had she married, were there more children? And his brother Credi – what was his situation? The question he wondered about most was whether Kathy had carried his child to term or not. Would it be unreasonable to assume the name could be Codona? He rarely thought of his own father Patrin, even though he believed that, 'He was a good man, my father, a good man.'

Strasbourg was a beautiful big busy and cosmopolitan city that rang no family search bells for Jonathan, and thus he needed to move on to other towns and countries in the search for historical family knowledge. The term gypsy, or Roma, brought no distinctive information to the surface and the local guide was no help in that area. EU countries were easy to move through freely using his Australian passport and the same modus operandi. So, move on he did. He knew that his best target countries were Romania and then perhaps Bulgaria, if still required. Visas were necessary but he was confident that his current identity was solid enough to protect him from any of the old hysteria or desire for revenge that may still exist, though he remained acutely conscious of the ever-present threat that existed from his old family connections. The employment of English-speaking aides or guides was dangerous only if he announced the surname of his target family. So, he concentrated on circus groups generally and the locality of their activities and residences. This was the long way around but in Jonathan's mind, the only way. He had a fair knowledge of the Romanian language from his family background, and recalled memories of childhood visits.

What he did discover that surprised him was the level of poverty and general dourness of large parts of the local population in Romania compared to that of Australia. But he also appreciated the beauty of the old buildings and towns. Careful use of his cash and contacts and staying very lowkey enabled him to attend events and shows and revive his use of the language to ask non-confronting questions. Having little luggage gave him the ability to move on quickly when necessary. As far as he was aware, he had attracted no notice from any law or police authorities. He decided his smartest action was to move quietly around Bucharest, the capital of Romania, as a tourist, making small sojourns to villages and sometimes to the city of Constanta about two hours away by car, making sure not to attract attention. He enjoyed what he was doing and appreciated more about Romania.

Jonathan thought he had been extremly careful in his investigations, in particular never using the name Codona in any instance. It was as well he had moved in that way, as somewhere along the way, within the 'Roma grapevine' it was recognised that someone, somewhere, was asking questions. Happily for Jonathan the first rumour was about a foreigner called David (thought to probably be a Kiwi) who had drunkenly got lost and admitted he was using a false name. Nothing came back to him.

Through his assortment of shell companies, Jonathan had a working knowledge of associates in Hells Angels bikie gang activities in the United States. He was aware that several gang members had been extradited from Romania to be tried in Texas on drug charges. Meth and cocaine were in high demand, and also cocaine from transported Peru to Texas, repacked and hidden in machinery, then sent on to Romania, then on to Australasia. Some of Jonathan's associates were involved and some product found its way into Australia. It was all highly convoluted, but seriously large sums of money changed hands and Jonathan was not 'super clean'; it gave him a reason to feel sightly on edge, even though he remained confident of his own security measures.

In the background, through intelligence from their counterpart the FBI in the US, the Australian Security Intelligence Organisation (ASIO) was beginning to put together a file on Jonathan Samuel Smithson. There were no obvious reasons at the moment but small murmurs sometimes lead to other solutions.

Jon was well aware that manipulation of a local drug market could often be controlled by one or two prison inmates with connections to senior members of crime gangs. Undercover drug enforcement agents in many countries were always active.

Chapter 39

DI Alexander: New Career?

With the death of Ron Brunton, what felt like a huge part of Linda's life within the police force ceased to exist. A long-term trusted senior associate and personal friend had been removed from a daily relationship. Almost at the same time, she was growing into a caring, loving relationship with an older man about whom she had as yet incomplete knowledge.

Her workplace was in regulated chaos as many and varied members of the force positioned themselves for their own futures. It seemed like nothing was going on, while yet everything was going on. Friends with years of service together were circumspect as they tried to seem neutral, as unofficial groups gathered and gossiped.

Linda had a reputation for integrity, honesty and loyalty but the position of Superintendent was a prized one and for many people, personal characteristics went out the door in some circumstances. Linda was finding this out! In earlier criminal cases, Linda had worked closely with members of the AFP, and she remembered on one celebrated occasion Superintendent Ron Brunton had 'warned off' his AFP counterpart from trying to recruit Linda. With the shenanigans that were developing over the selection panel methods,

Linda decided to refresh her memory of the activities and selection criteria that applied for the AFP. Quick and anonymous research disclosed the easy-to-meet initial basics:

Over 18 years,

Australian,

Valid driver's licence,

Negative vetting for security clearance,

Character standards.

Linda was not sure that her friend Ron would approve of her looking in this direction. Other detailed information about the nature of the work followed. Officers were expected to investigate and prevent crime to keep Australia and Australian interests overseas safe, and to that end:

Investigate such crimes that could and often did extend across state, territory and national borders,

Conduct complex investigations often with international partners,

Interview witnesses and suspects,

Make decisions on the appropriate law enforcement measures and collect, prepare, and present evidence to courts,

Collaborate with other teams within the AFP and with other police forces both at home and abroad.

The more Linda read, the more widely interesting it seemed to be. Was it a chance to make a difference, using personal integrity in a perhaps more challenging and active career with wider parameters?

She thought about her own qualifications and pathways: She was experienced in criminal investigations, intelligence, and had experience in forensics. She was sure she could meet the criteria expected of members. There were pathways within more than 200 role types, including base uni graduates, moving up into specialist roles, and also support personnel.

A required PCA (Physical Competency Assessment) fitness test was not a problem for her, she felt. The information she could obtain was all very interesting to her but of course did not provide any answers to the question, "What is the workplace like?" The literature on this point said: 'Challenging, rewarding, diverse, inclusive, supportive and fair.' A lot to consider.

Linda wanted to discuss the ramifications at home with Jonathan first, and no doubt he would have much to report on his visit to Europe and in particular Romania.

Amongst all these complications and work 'madness', was it appropriate for her to sometimes be rolling around in her head the subject of their possible marriage?

Chapter 40

Jonathan Smithson: True Confessions

As Jonathan was traipsing around several European countries, he was mindful of the need to give serious consideration to how or even why he needed to make full disclosures of his hidden and current activities to Linda. He was aware that sometime, he needed to disclose details of his chequered family history and past adventures to her. He also needed to explain the many illegal activities related to his wealth, both current and historically. Some things he would never admit to, such as visits to Soweto, negotiations with chiefs in Swaziland and other places that went awry with the result of physical violence being involved.

Unbeknown to Jonathan, some red flags has been raised from his careful visit to Europe. But keen not make any waves with his digging, he decided to leave more aggressive searching until he was back hidden in Australia. His holiday-type adventures had also brought back to him memories of some of his escapes and near capture when hastening from country to country when still under twenty years of age.

One memory in particular that came to him was his first experience with a prostitute in the back streets of Biarritz in south-west France. Then virtually penniless, sleeping on or around the beautiful Basque beaches, the odd job giving him just enough to eat one meal a day. A young street girl chatted to him offering various sexual services which he had never heard of. His total sexual experience up until then had been with cousin Kathy on a warm, loving basis. A price agreed, she led him to a scruffy little room off a badly-lit cobblestone lane and immediately started to undress. Jumpers with elbows out, scant smelly underclothes, and both under the one weak light bulb—they looked like scarecrows. She had his trousers down by his ankles and he touched her breast and ran a finger over her collarbone. One attempted kiss, pulled away, and that was it. He gave her the only money he possessed for what had been a very quick and ordinary experience. The question had to be, how much of this type of adventure, let alone his other activities and history, to disclose to Linda?

Homewood bound, Jonathan thought deeply about this, and decided to make preliminary notes for some things that might be discussed, to try to qualify subjects—all with the knowledge that because of his deep affection (was it love?) they were only for her.

Most of his naturalness had been smothered in his life of hiding and any openness had been so deeply buried that now Jon had an ironic approach to life. He wanted to have a normal relationship so he could express love, and be free in an outside world that caused no pain.

He wrote in his notes, "My young adulthood was deeply affected by circumstances that I brought on myself, but were then expanded by circumstances beyond my control. I do love you and the last thing I want is to cause you pain. A full and open confession of all my misdemeanours somehow is beyond my ability. Much is repetitive and I have no intention of disclosing much of the 'dishonourable'. Do you think you can exist with that type of with-holding? You may be surprised to know that we are almost to the anniversary of our first intimacy. That probably surprises you. 'Who is keeping a record?' I can hear you say! Who needs a special present?"

On his way home to Melbourne, Jon decided to stop off in Hong Kong where he had nefarious contacts from connections in Australia that were very important to him in retaining anonymity, but to also have some fun. He organised research into brother Credi and cousin Kathy and paid some fees up front. These were real 'heavies' of organised crime syndicates he was dealing with.

In a lighter frame of mind, he reminisced over a drink or two while enjoying the spectacular sights of Hong Kong Harbour. How had a man with so much to hide become involved with a senior policewoman! He consoled himself with a quote, 'A clever man can hide and survive.' He knew he wanted to bare his soul to Linda whenever they made love, or even held hands with quiet enjoyment. His existence had been so silent, so secretive, in everything he did. Most of his activities had deep protections so that he could disappear in the night—vanish like a ghost if required.

So, he visited 'Hardmans' drinking den to relax, and met up with various members of his international crime syndicate.

Chapter 41

Linda and Jonathan

Internal competitiveness — career issues

Getting together again was a really exciting and enjoyable time in spite of the complications in their lives. Linda was very concerned about back stabbing from within the police, and Jonathan was very concerned about whether he had 'set the foxes alive' whilst in Europe.

They had never had a regular pattern to overnight stayovers, as there had not been any whiff of desperation in their behaviour patterns. This afternoon, their reunion was at Jonathan's penthouse, and started with a most unusual glass of special sherry that Jonathan produced from the back of a cupboard as a special reunion drink. They could hardly wait to exchange stories but more importantly touch each other. They said nothing as clothes were discarded, and hurried words spoken about talking later. "Soon," Jonathan gasped while still in his boxer shorts and T shirt, partly exposing old scars on many parts of his body.

He told her, "Linda, I've missed you in my life and in my bed! I missed your beautiful body and the warmth of holding you close. I love you, Linda."

Her reply in short gasps, "I know you do!"

Afterwards, when they were resting, Linda went on, "that makes it even more important for us to be frank and honest with each other. We are both at crossroads." Almost simultaneously, they both agreed they needed long blocks of time together to tell each of their stories, even though they did admit some details could not be properly recalled. Maybe some should not be, thought Jonathan.

Jon volunteered to go back to the extreme end of the spectrum, to his non-Australian experiences. To South Africa, as that was where a part of his wealth had been created. To parts of his childhood, where his character had been moulded. He disclosed his real name, Hanzi, and that he had been in a US circus family of Romanian heritage. He told Linda stories including that he had long spells when he 'daydreamed' with an absent look on his face, which his mother called 'the faraways', and that his only close friend then was his cousin Katarina, whom he called Kathy. He explained how they plotted together to run away when he was 18 and she was pregnant, but this was stymied by the family before they could board the ship together, and Hanzi bolted from the US with a bounty on his head.

He gave no real details of his early ramblings from port to port in the UK, always looking over his shoulder to make sure he was not being followed. Then on to Europe—and here he made only some very vague references to doing 'casual work'—culminating in his arrival in Istanbul. He commented on Istanbul being the 'hub' of far eastern Europe and both exciting and dangerous. He was just a boy still at the time, but involved on the periphery in drug running for some heavies who did not even want to know his name. They were vicious low-level criminals with no consciousness of evil.

This time in Istanbul did, however, give him an awareness of the city's beautiful and incredible Byzantine Hagia Sophia grand mosque at a very young age. His appreciation of wider European history grew all the time. The emergence of Turkey as a critical geographical location was just beginning, but Jon's having Gypsy background was important to cover. He told Linda more about his family heritage in Romania.

Jon then moved on to a much closer date, in the late 1970s, when he arrived in South Africa with his new identity. He had arrived via numerous countries, endeavours and projects. Most importantly, he had with him a stash of money in varying currencies that local bank Nedbank appeared to accept with no concerns about where it had come from. The wheels seemed to be greased after Jon attended a meeting with a bank manager who was supporting a new eight-townhouse apartment development, which Jon and his connections were prepared to finance at just under one million Rand.

As he related all this to Linda, Jonathan explained the risk had been mainly his, but with a few persuaders and incentives, the project came in on time and under budget, and sold quickly, resulting in Jonathan more than doubling the investment for him and his connections, and accruing a high level of respect. He managed to make two more investments of a similar scale in and around Bryanstown, an upmarket northern Johannesburg suburb. There were conflicts of interest, but minimising problems had become a specialised skill for Jon and his associates. He said he learned to be friendly without having friends, lonely, with armour that could not easily be penetrated.

One casualty of Jon's life at this time that he told Linda about was a young woman who had become his assistant in his business deals. Her name was Mary and she also became his secret lover. In hindsight, he realised she had been a nymphomaniac, and, being what was termed a 'Cape coloured' woman, had many associated hangups and handicaps. He financially rewarded her as well as was possible under the circumstances but the relationship was doomed when she wanted more from him on a personal level. In giving the summary to Linda, he realised there were many associated emotional problems that he had never really considered.

Linda restrained herself from asking for more detail about what had happened, either then or now. On the surface she seemed to be taking it all in her stride. Her initial comment with a smile was indicative, "A police person's lot is neverending!" With more feeling she added, "I don't want to be alone any more. I'm not a solitary person. I don't know what single people do. I'm not designed to live alone!"

Linda was trying to be open emotionally and arrived to another of their 'open heart' sessions with tears only just suppressed. Unofficially, she had been told that her application for the Superintendent's position had not been successful. She was shattered by the earliness of the leak and the casual way it had been passed on to her. She considered she was entitled to deeper interviewing, explanation and perhaps counselling about the disappointment. Such communication did come a few days later, accompanied by the assurance she was to retain her current rank and status.

Jon was as angry as she was about her disappointment, but as he had experienced unexplained disappointments in hundreds of situations all over the world, he was more used to dealing with it. He commiserated with her, held her tightly and warmly, and encouraged her to 'let it all out'. The bastards! He helped her to recall every known profanity ever uttered. Linda was totally disenchanted now with Vic Police as she had endured a wide range of harassment during her career, and more recently around the Superintendant's position with anonymous notes being left on her desk or on her computer designed to warn her off. Awful examples such as, "Retarded Bitch! Don't apply; we don't want Sudi Africans! Men are better police! We know where you live! We know your boyfriend!"

She mentioned her research into the AFP to Jon. He suggested a short period of reflection before she took any action, as he was very aware his own position may not necessarily be that secure from that direction.

By way of distraction, Jonathan suggested sharing a bottle of Shiraz and a pizza in the park, a great location for him to confess some of his spicier parts of his story, and there he told her some of the story of his long journey to Australia, and to becoming Jonathan Smithson. He sometimes wondered whether, with his early childhood, wide travels and adult experiences, the saying attributed to the great Greek philosopher Aristotle of 'Give me a child until he is seven and I will show you the man' could be attached to him. Along the same lines, 'Give a child a place, a society, for the first seven years of life and he will be forever impressed, for better or worse, with what he sees, senses, and hears there.' Jonathan's recent travels through Europe had stirred in him many memories and feelings about, 'Where his real home was?'

At the same time, Linda had become energised by the apparent failure of her application for the position of Superintendent. She was furious, mainly by the methodology used. She was forced to reflect on the internal police culture, real or imagined. The petty sniping from some of her associates had at first bemused her, then infuriated her. Comments like, "Lindy, you would not be able to handle a hunk with his trousers down (from male officers) or uglier taunting, "Best to bring your girlfriend along" (from homophobic accusers about sexuality). Many were caught between male chauvinism or misogyny. No matter that this type of sly comment arose from jealousies held by only tiny numbers, it still did exist within the culture.

She immediately looked up every bit of information about methods and contacts she had at the AFP, anyone she could trust to give her insights into culture and morale within the organisation. She was hot under the collar enough to also conduct confidential research into the world of private investigators.

The first thing she discovered was the need for a licence to be issued by the Licensing and Regulation Division of her own Victoria

Police. This required meeting specific criteria, background checks and character references. How then to become, at her current level, part of a new successful team? Personal reputation was quite a different subject and very important. This made Linda address her own 'self- assessment' for any new or ongoing career.

Linda and Jon agreed that amid all the angst, the heightened personal warmth, and reassurances that there was a good case for Linda to fight the failure of her promotion application, she should 'just cool it' for now. To wait awhile before exploring possible other avenues.

Chapter 42

Jon and Linda: More Personal Disclosures

Linda called Beth to arrange a get-together so she could give her best friend an up-to-date emotional summary. The first question she posed of Beth was, "Well, what is your honest opinion of Jon? Warts and all."

Beth's response was, "Only an observation, as we have only met on a couple of occasions: he seems very nice and very private. Would you like me to do some private research? You well know I can keep secrets! It may be interesting." Linda chuckled, and they chatted about personal emotions, and Linda went on to summarise Jon's background as given by him, but with a rider that she was anticipating learning more from him over the next few weeks.

On the police situation, Beth gave very serious advice saying, "Do not resign or even make noises about resigning until any further circumstances, both good or bad, have evolved. As they say, 'keep your powder dry' for now!" They talked together about family and friends and agreed to meet more often as changes happened.

Over the next few days, Jon, giving out more occasional intimate comments, admitted to having business arrangements in the Virgin Islands and Dubai. He covered it over in generalities such as, "I have practised and learned to get away with things as necessary!"

In Dubai, he told Linda, the powerful leaders were domiciled on complete floors of upmarket hotels.

He admitted he had done business of sorts with associated gang leaders, and had always protected himself using his own shell companies. This alone was a huge disclosure for Jon to make. He also admitted that in Melbourne he had disguised interests in boxing gyms and wholesale importing companies. Money laundering in a very bland fashion was included in the generalities about his business affairs.

It was enough to make Linda very uncomfortable about who he really was, and her position as a senior police officer; what should she accept or tolerate? Exactly what illegality was he involved in? She was arriving at the conclusion he had interests in activities associated with the illicit tobacco trade, which was so much bigger than many appreciated. Her previous involvement in cracking open a large interstate cartel had given her the knowledge that heavy pressure was applied in this activity at all levels, right down to ownerships of retail stores. Did she love him so much that she could overlook his illegal activities? Could she—did she want to—spend the rest of her life with him?

Jon was totally in love in both a physical and emotional way that he was aware encouraged him to be dangerously outgoing, contrary to most of his adult life. He knew he was taking a big risk with his relationship with Linda. The sharing of his secrets created much self- imposed stress. To ease the pressure, it was common for him now to get into his tracksuit and runners for a long hard run through the nearby parks and streets to the point of exhaustion. That helped to ease his 'soul', refresh his mind, charge his batteries, clear his loneliness and conscience. He was very much in love with Linda but very stressed too.

Linda had dilemmas of her own. The seniority and ranks within the police force starting from Chief Superintendent down through

Deputy Superintendent, and Assistants to Chief Superintendent was complicated enough, and being a current senior Detective Inspector added to any future promotional aspirations. But missing her first tilt at promotion to Superintendant had thrown unexpected confusion into Linda's life. She was unsettled by both the internal and external circumstances she was dealing with. She was quietly very proud of the level she had achieved and occasionally gave thought to the extra degrees and diplomas she had worked hard for and the various police awards for successful arrests over the years. Naturally, she discussed her innermost thoughts and opinions with Jon, this all adding to the trust building up between them.

Jonathan became increasingly aware of the steps and sacrifices Linda had made to reach her current position. He was reluctant to tell her more of his past and family relationships, and omitted to elaborate on a casual, low-key 'friendship' with a high-level business executive in Melbourne. This particular man had never been admitted to the prestigious Club Melbourne, so he used his financial and commercial strength to become a member of the more rambunctious Savage Club, where he was respected and had many friends and contacts. Jon had been an invitee on one occasion, and their commercial relationship was much deeper and international than he was prepared to admit to anyone.

It came as a huge surprise to Jonathan and caused him some trepidation when he read in the local Melbourne morning paper, 'Drug Bust Scoops Luxuries'. What caught his eye was the address in Brighton, the description of a 46-year-old man, and the list of the products seized: cocaine, methylamphetamines, cash, BMW car, Ducati motorbike, Rolex and Tag Heuer watches. All linked to some storage facilities in Port Melbourne.

Detectives stated the drugs had been smuggled into Australia using postal services, among other methods detected by Border Force officers. It was easy for Jonathan to confirm among his business contacts that it was indeed his erstwhile 'friend' from the Savage Club. It was clear to him that the various police forces from different levels and countries had become much more sophisticated and were increasingly determined to track down the various 'Mr Bigs'.

Amid the efforts being made with Linda on honesty in their talks, Jonathan often wrestled with how far to go, as they individually tried to assess 'shared true values'. More and more Jonathan enjoyed the touch of her hand, the warmth of the rub against her body, and their special emotional connection. But he asked himself again, "Where is my real home, where is my real family?"

Protecting his confidentiality was still his overriding concern even though he trusted Linda.

However, he now often felt a compelling emotional curiosity about his child, whom he instinctively thought of as a girl. How old would she be now? Is she a Codona? How much Codona history should he own up to?

The personal relationship between them was advancing well as they both found more time to spend together. But both were holding back on unreserved total emotional commitment. Linda because, from the ongoing 'dripfeed' of life details released by Jonathan, she was becoming a little suspicious of his full and real identity, and Jonathan because of his reservations about revealing his history to a policewoman.

Their park walks were times of tranquillity and warmth both physically and emotionally. The familiarity and increasing lack of reservation about most subjects made time pass easily. The weekends in Jon's country house in Malmsbury were relaxing too. Not quite considering themselves 'middle-aged' yet, the two walked close together with hands often touching and holding, and lots of touches on the back and round the waist to make changes in direction. These pleasant times usually concluded with a coffee in one of the local cafés and quite often a move into Linda's apartment. It was smaller and cosy and comfortable, whereas Jonathan's apartment was more minimalistic and clinical.

Lovemaking was totally enjoyable for both in different ways. Linda had admitted to herself she had given her heart to Jon. She loved what she could see of him and what she knew they were to do. They both undressed at a relaxed speed, with Linda experiencing the tingles, the excitement, the anticipation of penetration, the vocalisation of enjoyment, and the total thrill of their lovemaking. Mature, comfortable and each time a pleasure.

For Jon, it was always no holding back but a less lingering high. It was consensual sex in its fullest form. The slow and deliberate undressing made it even better. The soft sounds of popular and classic music tones in the background made the event more enjoyable.

Having never been married or having children, Linda was not fully aware of the complexities in Jonathan's mind when he dwelt on thoughts of his parents and unknown daughter.

He had found out through his connections that Kathy had married and left the US, and his parents were deceased. Older brother Credi was now the senior family member. It was painful to think that he may never see Credi or Kathy again, but overriding that emotion was the knowledge that any foolishness in the form of an attempt to reunite could create great danger for him.

Chapter 43

Linda and Jon: Unease About True Commitment

Linda.

Despite her increasing intimacy with Jon, Linda found there were ever more questions building in her mind. Walking in the park together, weekends in the country, sharing books, watching movies, quoting poetry aloud together, attending the occasional show at the nearby theatres in the CBD or inner suburbs, and most recently exchanging a spare set of door keys to each other's apartments… These things reflected their huge leap in mutual trust. However, Linda could not help thinking about the questions she now had, and on the occasions she was in Jon's apartment had noted that the spare room there was actually always locked.

Linda was being made acutely aware of the lack of integrity and shortcomings that human beings could exhibit, highlighted by the jockeying going on surrounding the internal promotions within the Victorian Police Force. The main 'rock' in her relationships, apart from her family and Jon, was Beth Jenkins. They met regularly and it was clear to Beth that Linda was still sometimes quite naïve both commercially and emotionally. Her simple inner strength was boosted by her uncomplicated childhood, quality education, simple and regular financial investments in her police superannuation, and her low-cost, low-key lifestyle. A career police woman, she had no religious background or connections, few interests outside the police, and had had few real sexual adventures.

Linda was, though, a very efficient senior member of an elite detective group in the Victoria Police, and as such played the part and looked the part. Her usual dress did not vary much from her uniform of black calf-length skirt, plain white neatly fitting blouse, and black jacket. Her hair was pulled back and tied behind the ears for work, and she wore mid to low-heeled black shoes. She usually carried a black leather briefcase. She liked to think she dealt in facts, and believed that people generally liked and respected her. She tended to think that everyone else was like her.

Sometimes she took a little time to consider her age in biological terms, and realised she and Jon had never discussed having a baby.

VicPol's successful recent drug bust had involved a 46-year-old businessman from Brighton named Darryl Cornwell, This had been a triumph for international cooperation against the ever-growing drug trade by Australian crime syndicates worth millions of dollars on the streets. Linda and her team were an integral part of this success.

Jonathan.

Mounting complications began to form in Jonathan's mind. Also rolling around was a plan to conduct further digging into the situation of his daughter Maria and even her parents Kathy and Alessandro, known now to be in Romania. Love, disappointment, anger, revenge and other emotions related to his family bubbled unbidden to the surface sometimes. He wondered what his daughter would look like. Where, when and how might he be able to meet them in person, in an atmosphere of love or friendship? Jonathan was well aware there was absolutely no prospect of uniting the old with the new. He did not want to involve Linda in the necessary activities if he chose to search again.

Jonathan had the capability to easily undertake a full-blown investigation but something was restraining his actions. His strength was both financial and in his anonymity. He had no strong feelings of guilt and his mental strength added to his emotional wellness. He was reluctant to acknowledge the origins of his wealth, however. For this reason Jon was reluctant to ever pose the question to anyone else about the acquisition of their wealth.

Unbeknown to him, other organisations were posing those questions. He had acquired friends and admirers along the way— unintentionally—by virtue of the way he had conducted his business relationships. A quandary? Not really, as respect can be earned, even as he stayed a little aloof. What could possibly go wrong? Jon knew it could be too much exposure to associates in crime.

Jonathan often enjoyed breakfast at upmarket neighbourhood hotels, either the Pullman or right next door at the Sofitel. At both hotels, he was recognised and treated with respect. In comparison to Linda's light, early breakfasts at home, his routine was a full breakfast that started with coffee delivered to his table, his own selection from juices, cereals and fruit at a leisurely pace. He would then order bacon, eggs, tomatoes and mushrooms. Toast and butter with marmalade in small quantities, with another coffee to follow and always the newspaper to leisurely read. Then daily workouts at his building's gym.

Jon read about Darryl Cornwell in the newspaper, but did not spare a thought for his welfare as he considered himself to be fully insulated from him. He did wonder though what he might do to further strengthen his position. More importantly, he decided it was time to give thought to a 'Plan B' and make sure he was fully up to speed with the technology available to avoid any pursuers. In the most extreme circumstance, what would be the trigger to embrace an alternative action, and would this action possibly include 'suicide'?

He reflected that he was not really lonely; one of his strengths, and something that had been pivotal in keeping him undiscovered all these years, was his comfort with solitude and his memories. However, his growing intimate relationship with Linda could be akin to a growing trap that he may need to modify.

Chapter 44

Jon's Trip Overseas

Thoughts of family, of Kathy and her child, kept nagging away in Jon's head and the continuing curiosity got the better of him. Without telling anyone, not speaking to Linda first, he booked a tentative return flight to Romania for a short visit in the near future. Using his most trusted arm's-length contacts, he precipitated a search for signs of recent family activity in Romania. He asked that the contacts concentrate on the Codona name, any Cordona records, and any changes in the status of Katarina and Alessandro and Maria. The need for extreme caution and confidentiality were naturally underlined. Jonathan also stressed that if investigations in another country were justified, that could be approved. In setting this research in motion he felt nervous, but he ordered that it get underway anyway. While away he would take the time for a visit to Turkey as well, as he wanted to again visit the Hagia Sophia Grand Mosque in Istanbul—it was a 'must' to visit on any occasion.

Jon's input to his overseas contacts included that Bucharest would be well worth a search and circuses and funfairs most likely a good start. Kathy and Alessandro's status could still be under the surname Codona, but their lifestyle could be consistent with a Gypsy background. Katarina may now have a first different name if she was performing as a star in a circus. They could have emigrated to almost any country, but had chosen Romania for family connections and a good working future. Romania and Bulgaria have by far the biggest concentrations of Gypsy populations in Europe.

A serious question for Jonathan regarding Linda had to be, "What must finally come out, and what do I keep to myself?"

He wanted to connect with Katarina, and he wanted to tell her what he had done and become. He wanted to imagine her in person now, and he wanted to outline to her his adventures. He looked in a mirror and thought he looked very tired. He now felt guilt about leaving her behind with the baby, and was sure she would never want to see him and hear his story, no matter how he softened it.

Chapter 45

Retrospective

Linda was aware of the unsettled situations encompassing both of them. Her own position in the police force seemed to be hanging in the balance, and Jonathan was clearly very unsettled, even to the point of talking about a 'Plan B', that they should both singularly and together be working on! For that reason alone, Linda was very concerned. It was reassuring for her that although Jonathan was single, it appeared he had no interest in other women, though she was unaware he now badly wanted to contact Katarina, and to tell her about his life since they last saw one another. In his mind, he emphasised repeatedly the feeling, "My own daughter! For God's sake, someone has to tell her our story!"

Is blood thicker than love?

Through Beth, Linda became aware of the mounting concentration of police resources being expended on overseas criminal syndicates and snippets arising from that which could perhaps suggest a connection to Jonathan. Was the AFP involved or simply had some historical connection?

One afternoon Linda was at home, reflecting on her own family relationships and how simple and transparent they were as she looked through old photos. Sacrifices aplenty but easy to justify and easy to talk about. She noted to herself that she had never seen or discussed any of Jon's personal memorabilia.

Everyone has a need for someone or something to trust in. Even the most evil men love someone and someone loves them. Whether this fact was liked or not, Linda considered it to be true. For most, sacrifices have been worth it.

Linda and Jon's closeness was growing as each day went by and they shared interests in things such as music, books and movies. Their movie interests were wide, stretching back to old ones with Humphrey Bogart such as 'Casablanca', 'African Queen', and many others, including 'The Caine Mutiny', and encompassing the serious criminality of 'The Godfather' series and more light-hearted enjoyment from the Bee Gees movies and music. Their book interests were much more eclectic, but neither followed sports or sporting heroes. Only Linda had a real interest in poetry. Jonathan tried hard. A single verse from school that kept bouncing to the front of Linda's brain was the final verse of 'To Althea, from Prison':

> 'Stone walls do not a prison make,
> Nor iron bars a cage;
> Minds innocent and quiet take
> That for a hermitage;
> If I have freedom in my love,
> And in my soul am free;
> Angels alone that soar above
> Enjoy such liberty.'

With great honesty, Jonathan finally admitted to himself, "I can't do this much longer — I really can't." He qualified his ongoing insistence in his own mind by thinking, "You have to go off the beaten path sometimes; it does a person good."

Then out of the blue came the news he was hoping for. Katarina Codona had been located!

Chapter 46

Jon in Bucharest, and Katarina

The exciting news from his overseas contacts arrived via the usual several levels. The discovery was apparently made in Bucharest, and as expected covered with some mild subterfuge. If it was correct, she was using a different surname but she still using the given name Katarina, sometimes Kathy. It was part of her determination to escape from the old and bitter family histories. Having travelled extensively, she knew where she could be comfortable.

Katarina was a now mid-level school teacher essentially teaching English to 10 -to -12-year-olds in Bucharest. Alessandro was working in an engineering factory, manufacturing components for motor vehicles. They had one female child still living at home. They both had connections with administrative part-time roles with a small circus.

Jonathan immediately leapt into action to activate his booked flight. It was not well planned or thought out, but he made an appointment to see the private investigator in Bucharest to examine the information collected. He did not consult Linda, beyond giving her a quick resume of his emotions and still professing to love her. He explained the trip by saying he had a business interest to meet.

He was not aware that his various trips to mid-Europe were

throwing up some red flags in AFP security areas. Even if he were to realise such a thing was happening, he still held the opinion that he had done nothing criminal that could be discovered.

On arrival in Bucharest and sitting down with the private investigator, he was pleased to find she spoke adequate English and even when she broke into Romanian, he could understand the words she used. Jonathan wanted to be convinced of the accuracy of her information and wanted to see photographs. One child of around sixteen years old lived at home and another older child, apparently an adult, lived elsewhere.

It seemed obvious that Katarina was now living a very ordinary lifestyle as a teacher in a communist dictatorship. Did he really want to disrupt that just for his own gratification? From all the side investigations he could make, it was confirmed that this was in fact, 'his' Katarina Codona. Was he within his rights to further investigate this family's life and financial position?

So, his only known family was living very much a lower middle class existence in a country where heating still came from wood fires and life probably encompassed a level of day-to-day fear of authorities. It probably meant life was fairly sombre and dull, with people holding no great expectations for the future. He placated his uneasy state of mind by repeating an old saying, "in spite of everything, life goes on. It always does."

Observing every possible means to retain his anonymity including a severe verbal caution to his guide/researcher, Jon set about finding out as much as possible about Katarina. He finally sighted her, and with a shock saw that she was now a plump, dowdy, middle-aged woman, looking older than she actually was; seemingly neither happy or unhappy. She owned an old Skoda car, left mainly on the street. He felt no immediate compulsion to seek a face-to-face meeting, and discarded any ideas that might have been lurking in the back of his imind or anonymous gifts or rescue plans for the family to migrate to Australia, or indeed any attempt to reunite. In fact, this all sealed his wish to return to Australia to sit and talk with Linda to try to outline their own future.

He now admitted to himself he needed to make a full acknowledgement to Linda of his history, marriage and child. He hoped he could include some of his more erratic past behaviour. He realised he was now on the cusp of the next stage of his life.

Part of his own makeup included the philosophy that was he was subject to outside influences such as karma and fate.

Before returning 'home' to Australia, he decided on a few days sightseeing around favourite cities and even a few places from childhood days. Naturally, his mind often stretched to the welfare, whereabouts and health of his own child. He wanted to make an attempt to meet her. However, his contacts could not establish where she was. He decided to try again to find her in the future. His now cemented adult persona was able to restrain anything that could jeopardise his security.

Chapter 47

Jonathan: Homewood Bound

Jonathan was back in his own luxury apartment almost before Linda realised it. To her his first question was, "Well, what has happened while I have been away?"

A little testily Linda replied, "What have you done while away?" and then they morphed into the warmest cuddle and headed into bed. Two wonderfully warm and happy people to explore one another's emotions and bodies to the fullest, appreciating how much they had missed one another. Warm lips and exploring fingers into remote body spots as only more mature and quietly confident lovers can enjoy. Linda kept repeating, "I really missed you and kept wondering how it was all going."

Jonathan, a little guiltily, had to admit in his own mind that he had been so hell bent on his own project that he had not thought too much about what Linda might be doing, but it had helped him to come to some serious conclusions. Their lovemaking was long, warm and wonderful. They had a couple of repeat runs just to emphasise the sheer pleasure they could give each other.

That same morning, in the local Herald-Sun newspaper, a small item caught Jonathan's eye. "Mexican meth: 10kg discovered" read the headline. Detail followed announcing that two persons faced the prospect of years behind bars after the discovery of a haul of methamphetamine in a Fitzroy storage unit. Customs officers reported that a man and a woman were arrested after the meth, which had been imported from Mexico, had arrived via international freight and was tracked to the storage unit. After searches at their home in St Kilda, the man and woman were charged with possession of an extra 68kg of MDMA at their home and other charges involving the possession of a Mercedes-Benz, luxury watches, a pistol and quantities of cash. A third man, of no fixed address, was released pending further enquiries.

The significance of this newspaper report for Jonathan was that he recognised the probability of the St Kilda address being that of an associate of one of his remotely held shell companies who operated on a basis of 'procure to order' products for third party usage or export.

This small report sent shivers up the Jonathan's spine about possible ramifications. Without any waste of time, he went to his apartment's locked room, opened his substantial office safe and pulled out onto his desk a range of highly confidential documents to remind himself of the various connecting investments he held at arm's length in various countries that safeguarded his wealth. The shiver he had felt also reminded him of the task he had set himself to 'tell all' — up to a point — to Linda. Could he still do that? How secure was he? What immediate risk was there by the arrest of the couple from St Kilda? Were his insulation arrangements fully secure? Totally non-traceable?

Chapter 48

Linda: New Assistant Superintendent Role

For Linda, huge news! The Police Commissioner had advised that it had been agreed to reopen applications for the role of Superintendent. More importantly the specifications for the position had been modified, and there were to be two new positions as responsibilities were to be divided:

Position 1. Assistant Superintendent.
This role was to report to the Commissioner, and would be responsible for local drug, gambling and alcohol offences. Policing closer to home where Linda was most experienced.

Position 2 Assistant Superintendent.
This role was to report directly to the Commissioner, and could cover syndicates and international crime.

The suggestion from on high was that Linda apply for Position 1. The first move she made was to call Beth to arrange an off-premises chat. Things like remuneration, status, super, etc were all readily available for examination. For Linda, the most important information needed was, "who was the actual person to whom she would be reporting in the Commissioner's office?" She still had lingering in the back of her mind the possibility of the AFP, or even ASIO. But another matter loomed ahead of all else, and before deciding whether to apply for the role, she needed to talk over the situation regarding Jonathan.

A small coffee shop in Spring Street, at the eastern end of the City, was their chosen venue, to talk over a quiet breakfast. Great friends can quickly get to the point. Beth asked, "Apart from me and family, do you have close social friends outside the force? If the answer is no, you're relying on Jon to fulfil the rest of your days, and maybe you're on thin ice there? Surely you are entitled to ask him for indepth disclosures if you are contemplating a long-term commitment?"

They talked back and forth, with no real resolution except it helped Linda to decide she must ask Jonathan for full disclosure about his life to reinforce her love for him. As she reflected, "Make peace with your past so it won't screw up the present."

Chapter 49

Was She Pushed? A Melbourne Mystery

The 000 call was answered promptly at Vic Police, "Details please." Panic in his voice and almost a scream, the person on the phone shouted, "Yes! This is the central Melbourne Fire Brigade in Albert Street, East Melbourne; there's been a terrible accident and an officer is down, there's blood everywhere!" Very calmly, the telephonist asked for full name and address with constant reassurances that officers would be despatched urgently.

"Please do not move anything, an ambulance is on its way. Can you give me full details of where the injured person is situated, please? "

"In the assembly hall next to where vehicles are despatched—Eastern Hill Fire Station".

This call received a full alert and a standard police van very close by with two uniformed officers was redirected, and at the Fire Station within four minutes. Full sirens and an ambulance one minute later.

They were taken immediately to the large assembly hall were the injured officer lay in full uniform but with no head gear. As had been called in, there was blood everywhere. She appeared to have a broken leg and ankle and had a big gash to the back of the head. It took no time at all for the ambulance team to announce the patient was deceased. Officials were scrambled in many directions. The police officers called in aid from their higher ranks as they perceived this could be a difficult and delicate case. It would certainly require the attendance of a forensic pathologist. After appropriate scene examinations had been made and photographs taken, police handed the body to the ambulance crew.

Detective Inspector Alexander was alerted and appointed to head the investigation, not least because of her seniority, but also because Linda's office was not more than a good stone's throw away. As the excitement settled down, the first question Linda had for Dr Westbury, Pathologist, was, "How are you William, and what have you got for me? Any idea of time of death yet?"

"Hi Linda,"he said. "Good to see you still on the job. Looks to be a violent crack on the back of the head, plus multiple physical injuries by a fall, maybe down the stairs. Reserve full answers until autopsy. There's vomit, which is suspicious and suggests the use of drugs, socially or otherwise. The closed location makes things easier."

Unofficial identification of the victim was easy as she was in uniform, though oddly without her boots, and at work. No need to search any missing persons list. It was Leading Firefighter Maeve Murphy, about thirty years old. Linda brought Detective Constable Alia Singh with her and asked her to collect a complete list of all staff and other people on the premises, stressing the need for sensitivity within the brigade membership Media exposure at this stage was to be minimised. Without admitting it out loud, Linda was delighted to be in charge of such a murder investigation with all the complications of membership, rank, discipline and public service all wrapped together, similar to the police. She asked for thoughts about likely cause or manner of death but no responses were anticipated.

A full schedule of meetings for all brigade staff was to be set and addressed by the Assistant Chief Fire Officer and DI Alexander. Linda would attend to be available to give general answers before routine questioning of individuals began. This would take place over several days. Linda hoped she had not lost any of the skills needed for the interviews and possibly interrogations that would follow.

Maeve Murphy was a young firefighter of Irish background. Like so many young people, she was lightly tattooed.

Was it murder or just an accident? Motive for murder? There were mixed initial opinions on this. Maeve was ambitious, skilled, meticulous, liked by higher ranks, disliked by lower ranks. One opinion offered was that she could be infuriating but also intriguing. She apparently had a narrow range of friends, and shared a flat with two 'non-Firey' female companions. Linda ordered a search warrant for her address.

The initial on-the-spot opinion from Dr Westbury was that accident seemed unlikely; there was probably more than one assailant involved because, judging by the awkwardness of the body position, the firefighter had been moved, and alcohol and or drugs could well have been involved because of the vomit in evidenc. Linda asked for a full forensic report as soon as possible.

"Yes! Yes! I know," answered Westbury patiently.

A full site inspection was carried out. DI Alexander put into place the necessary steps to begin the witness interviews, using the facilities provided by the Fire Brigade with absolute cooperation from them.

The first conversation was with Maeve Murphy's immediate superior, who had not been present on the night of the death. She had an undoubted alibi, but her comments were valuable. Linda asked about team bonds, honour, loyalty, any potential for a conspiracy of silence, and was assured that Maeve had fully respected the service traditions. Other ranks interviewed agreed that Firefighter Murphy was a competent team member.

From one of the routine questions, one interviewee commented, "Are you aware she is gay?

Linda answered, "No, but does it matter?"

The answer was, "No, but she does meet with all sorts and frequent some odd places." Others confidentially called her cheap and common. Linda thought to herself, "You can't please all of the people all of the time."

Linda was told that an earlier anonymous 'whistle blower' call had asserted the Maeve was 'too butch' and aggressive, was well known for name calling, and had a history of stealing minor pieces of male jewellery. None of these things had ever been reported. Was it honour of the brigade? Linda had initially thought the arrest of the guilty person would be comparatively easy. She also welcomed the input and energy from Constable Singh, who was on a steep learning curve.

Reports flowed in and thanks to answers from many firefighters, it was possible to establish there had been a 'threesome' of people on the premises the evening of the death.

Further questions established that one of the three was a 'non-Firey', and that there had been a guided tour of facilities, some noise and probably alcohol. Others suggested elements of jealousy. Linda used aggressive questioning to find out more as a non-approved walk-through had been done at the premises. The firefighter who was the third part of the threesome was identified, while a 'bring in' order was established for the non-Firey to be interviewed. She was one of the tenants in the apartment block where victim Maeve Murphy lived.

The 'third person' firefighter trembled violently during the interview and quickly confessed what had happened, with encouragement from the senior brigade officer who had been appointment as the official support. What had happened was that after a few drinks, and in a noisy and boisterous mood, they had decided to visit the brigade for an inspection to be conducted by their friend. Some old jealousies arose and after some pushing and shoving the non-Firey swung round and king-hit Murphy, who fell to the ground, crashing her head on the floor and immediately falling unconscious. It seemed she was dead and panic set in between the other two.

A ridiculous plan was hatched. Take the body into the assembly area and dump it by the bottom of the stairs. Hit her head with a brick, and escape. The shaken and trembling firefighter was adamant that she was no more than a witness aiding and abetting an accident. It was a frail excuse.

The pathologist's report was able to confirm the cause of death was loss of blood from the blow to the back of the head, and the time of death was between midnight and 1am. The search of the apartment offered no more help other than matching hair and a small amount of recreational drugs. Maeve Murphy's missing boots were discovered behind a truck as they had come off while the body was being dragged.

Linda assured Constable Singh that this was a murder, "not just another routine cog in the life of a police officer!"

Chapter 50

Jonathan: Closely Examining His Situation

Jonathan was uneasy. He had emailed his agent in Chicago and invited him to an unofficial meeting in Waikiki, Hawaii. He wanted the meeting in a private location with no links to either of them. A suggested agenda was to cover bland subjects like land purchase and tourism. He knew their real subjects would be investments, shell company protections, people involvements, security flexibility and asset convertibility.

The agent/lawyer was quick to agree to a flight to Oahu Island because his client was paying for it and he had always been intrigued with this mysterious man!

They met in an atmosphere of warmth and trust, and Jonathan Smithson, as he was now known, wanted to check on the various tentacles that existed in his investments, and the protections in place. He also wanted an update on the bounty on his existence. Without too much icing and just for the sake of appearances they covered the beauty of Honolulu and Maui beaches, then moved on to how thorough were the safeguards in place and would they cover his butt under every condition.

The lawyer arrived with a summary of all the transactions and investments known to him. These did not cover Jonathan's activities in southern Africa. Jonathan was concerned that the agent now knew his Australian identity, but total trust had existed for decades and Jonathan hoped it would continue unabated and that the guardrails he had established in Australia would still be sufficient.

A huge quandary for him now was what disclosures if any he could or should make to Linda, and how safe would that be if he did. He did not mention her name or occupation to the agent or ask for any guidance on that subject!

Chapter 51

VicPol Pressure on Linda

Superintendent Ron Brunton had been Linda's immediate boss for many years in VicPol and there had been the prospect she was a likely successor to his very senior role. His early death and the changing philosophies within the police force had changed many expectations. She had kept all her internal training and postgraduate diplomas up to date, and was well aware of 'the changing of the guard'. Forensic psychology was a fast-growing profession closely associated with the justice system. With the newly defined two positions to replace the old Superintendent's role, Linda was made aware that there would be an emphasis on 'local' criminality in the area she was encouraged to apply for. She would be interviewed and closely questioned by internal psychologists as well as senior members of the force.

The meetings and interviews were now about to begin. It was a time of stress and strain on her, and this was deepened by her relationship issues with Jon Smithson, and all the unanswered questions that still existed in her brain.

After Jon returned from Hawaii he and Linda agreed the time was 'now' for some real soul searching. They arranged to meet in their favourite coffee shop in the park for an in-depth talk on childhoods, experiences, and memories.

Chapter 52

Personal Disclosures
Jonathan opening up

For Linda it was easy to talk to Jon, as she had often spoken of her childhood in South Africa and the beautiful memories of her privileged upbringing and the huge changes brought to her whole family by their emigration to Australia. Her entry into university in WA, and the WA Police Force. Ninety percent of her memories were clear and pleasant. In the police she had had an enviable record of catching and prosecuting criminals of all levels, from murderers to tobacco retailer warfare. Inter-staff relationships had been on the whole amicable. She disclosed several prior personal relationships.

When it came to Jon's turn to give a summary, he knew it was going to be difficult. Linda's success was easy to relate and to be proud of. Personal relationships were equally easy to summarise as being short-term traumatic, but no long-term damage to those involved. She was now wanting to enter into a permanent relationship and was looking for a similar acknowledge from Jon. The word marriage had come up in their discussions.

But there were all those difficulties with Jon's identity. After examining the business organisation chart extracted from his locked safe, he knew that in realilty he could be labelled as a 'Mr Big'. So he decided that he would still give Linda only a limited summary. Recently, he had taken the decision to send an anonymous amount of money to his daughter Maria, against advice. However, this turned out not to be a problem, because in a very vigorous and even hostile way the gesture was rejected with a note "no wish to know who the donation is from!"

Rather vaguely, he covered the circumstances of his early relationship with his cousin Katarina Codona that set the family henchmen on his trail. How he initially became a desperado of sorts, fake name, doing casual work, hiding from imaginary shadows, travelling through numerous countries in Europe, sleeping in doorways and on beaches on many nights or in low-cost doss houses, earning cash for jobs and occasionally being robbed!

His first step into maturity was the period with the French Foreign Legion, which in hindsight had been his saving. A boy with no name maturing into a fully respected man with rank in a highly trained fighting army. Adventures as an enthusiastic 'soldier of fortune' beginning to build his character, experiences and wealth. Mastering the ability to write and speak French, and building the desire for more education—thanks to the French Foreign Legion.

His single-minded application to the pursuit of anonymity—and wealth—in many developing countries had not been without personal casualties and erosions of integrity. Some not-so-pleasant memories. His new name and the creation of an entire folio of personal records that cost large sums of cash involved dishonest transactions in South Africa. Jon had often reflected then about 'No base, no stability'. He was, though, able to begin with new bank accounts and holdings of significance that added to his powers of persuasion and the creation of his new persona.

Jonathan skimmed on through his story from there. Now and again, he told of flashbacks of half-remembered childhood family relationships in the US, and trips abroad with grandparents—scattered smiles and warmth. He thought of some words from a song sung by Paul Robeson in a deep, deep voice, that seemed apposite: "Old man River, that old man river…; he just keeps rolling along."

He decided his days in various countries in southern Africa were better for minimisation, as that was where he had begun to form his host of shell companies with trusts and tentacles to hide ownership. This required an array of registrations and legal administrative arrangements, and anonymity in several countries including Swaziland, Tanzania, Mozambique, Zimbabwe and Namibia. Fertile ground for enterprising activities. One of his connections was into the dangerously wild and lawless commercial arena of drugs, in particular in Syria and Lebanon, where risk and violence go hand in hand. Here he was an early participant.

The abbreviated summary Jon gave to Linda was spread over several long walks, over coffees, and over glasses of Shiraz in their favoured locations. He made no mention of possible desperados on his trail nor law enforcement authorities in different states or countries. His emphasis was on the present. He did accentuate a certain wealth status that applied to him. In talking about his own personal happiness, he went to great lengths to stress his awareness of the fragility of love and the importance of a permanent relationship—marriage. He indicated he believed he had the maturity, when considering the constant togetherness that can bring to the surface attitudes that could be all of confronting, painful, rewarding, hilarious, exposing and wonderfully romantic, to handle all situations. He understood the need to wrap together the multiplicity of factors in their relationship.

Jon wanted to stress her position as an enforcer of the law and his position on the fringes of it. He had accepted that he was in fact a style of Mr Big even though he was practically anonymous, as much of his decisionmaking had harmful ramifications all around the world. But could she accept this about him? Jon's prime effort was to engage Linda in explanations as to why she could or should embrace the total commitment they were contemplating. He knew all he needed to know about her, given by her with complete trust, but was her trust in him justified? That was the question.

So, he asked her, "Linda my love, this is probably the most serious question I have ever asked you; do you have absolute unqualified trust to live with me for the rest of our lives?"

Hesitation, as his indeterminate position on the wrong side of the law still worried at the back of her mind, but love was love, and she was tired of being on her own. "Yes, I do!" she replied firmly.

To celebrate, they booked themselves into the Sofitel Hotel for an evening meal and accommodation even though it was right next door to home, and for the first time their booking was made together with no need for constraints. A really great occasion.

Chapter 53

Small Car Accident: Distraction?

Time is a great leveller. For Linda, it slipped by quickly as she wrestled with police protocol and all the detail and routine associated with her new appointment. It was exciting and formidable, but she also wondered at times whether it was the right decision for her.

In no time her relationship with Jonathan had reverted to the steady, comfortable, moderate behaviour from weeks back. However, she could not help noting that they were nowhere near as intimate as they used to be. She assumed that Jon would reply in a jocular manner if she raised this—'nobody in the history of partnerships had ever been as intimate as we used to be!' However, Linda kept reflecting, "I'm tired—tired of the same comments about career, health, wealth, security, and dreams." That surprised her, and gave Jon a jolt when she broached the subject in her modest way to him.

In his turn, Jon had been quietly examining his personal dilemma of what to do about daughter Maria—leading to sleeplessness and a heightened sense of unease. He also had growing concerns about the activities of some of his minions in Australia and overseas, perhaps indicating a need to be more active in hiring and firing. The still-standing bounty and the security of his US legal protection was always with him, and his ties to overseas organised crime syndicates, with their connections filtering into Australia, were always there for him to consider.

Strange how little things can mean a lot. Jonathan was driving his second car, a luxury Lexus SUV, in Melbourne, when he absent-mindedly turned left at a set of lights when the arrow to the left was red, but the straight-through light was green. In turning, he knocked over a 'suit' waiting on his bicycle. It was clearly an expensive bike, and some minor damage had been sustained to the handlebars. No one was hurt but in the ensuing discussion, the suit became angry. No major damage, said Jonathan, and no one's hurt. But the man became angrier and raised his voice. Jonathan told him to grow up. There were witnesses, demands for identification and talk of repairs. A smallish incident, but the victim was determined to pursue the matter. He demanded Jonathan's name, took the registration of the Lexus and asked who the insurer was. This small event turned acrimonious. Days went by until a legal letter arrived demanding a large amount for damages. It had clearly been a quality bicycle, with the letter including details of purchase price. Jonathan declined to answer as the sheer size of the damages amount he thought ludicrous. However, witnesses had confirmed definite error by the driver, and some ensuing arrogance.

A series of events ensued, including a formal complaint to Vic Police. Jonathan had no police record and the car was owned by a small, nondescript company. It should have stopped there but the angry victim insisted on "more police action". What it did was to raise a question within the police about Jon Smith—who was he and had he ever before come to their notice? Their enquiries revealed that Jonathan Smithson owned another car: It was his pride and joy that he kept very quietly in a rented garage in Brunswick. It was a 1967 Jaguar Type 3.4-litre Manor Park Classic. Sparkling Silver, spoke wheels, light fawn upholstery, sun roof, manual with overdrive. A collector's car. Jonathan thought to himself that he was pleased it was only the Lexus involved and not the Jaguar! However, the complaint went on police files.

Linda noticed a change in Jonathan's moods, both as she pursued her aims within the police force and his apparent distraction on more personal events at home and abroad. Their discussion level seemed to have declined. She did not know about the rented property in Brunswick or the classic car.

Amid this unsettled atmosphere, a tipoff emerged that involved Detective Senior Sergeant Beth Jenkins and her division, related to enquiries about burglaries and arson taking place in suburban retail stores. It seemed young criminals were stealing cars and ramraiding premises for selected products, then destroying the cars and presumably delivering the goods to a 'mastermind'. Great pressure was applied and one of the more senior 'kids' (about 18 years old) admitted he received his instructions from a bikie gang member who in turn was given targets and products wanted. The tipoff was that these instructions came from much higher up, from an apparent 'cleanskin', and this person was an immigrant.

The kids thought it was great fun and they were almost Teflon-coated, because even if they were locked up it was only for a minimal time because of their young ages, and they were rewarded with big cash. The level of violence was escalating, however, as were the number of requests for arson. And the danger. Beth and her crew were getting closer to the criminal elements operating the system. Internal information from a rival bikie gang helped them to arrest some participants and glean more accurate detail of participants. Experience from the past with tobacco and alcohol across borders made Beth well aware of the size of the activities and nature of crooks involved in illegal trading; a very big business! A special new division called the Special Action Group—lamentably quickly becoming widely referred to by its acronym "SAG"—was set up with Beth Jenkins as senior officer.

Chapter 54

Empire...

Crumbling. Tumbling.

Linda began to work closely with Beth's SAG unit, and enjoyed the thrill of success as each little part of the bigger crime group was identified. In some ways she felt this was 'real' policing instead of office and bureaucracy that had filled her days more recently as appointments were being finalised. She loved it.

Jon made a decision to secretly explore offshore a method he could utilise to try making another anonymous payment to his daughter in Budapest. He knew the idea was dangerous and his confidential legal adviser warned him against it, but his ongoing mental worries and less relaxed relationship with Linda made him keen to investigate the idea. A little event like the persistent action from the bicycle rider he had hit had made his tolerance even lower. He spent a disproportionate amount of time thinking about possible ways to make donations and even formation of companies using her name. It became obvious he was pushing into a dangerous area, which did not help his underlying mental state or his temper. Naturally, Linda noticed his change. She mentioned it to Beth, who in turn commented to her about the 'skirmish' that she knew Jonathan was having over a small vehicle accident.

Then Jon received a communication from his agent in Chicago telling him that he was retiring, and that they had just received a new enquiry about the bounty from a distant Codona family relation. Ms Anita Pearson from within the Chicago firm was taking over all clients. Changes of this nature made Jonathan nervous. The mounting circumstances helped him decide to confess to Linda a range of personal details he had not previously felt able to.

So finally, after much conversation over a glass or two of wine in Linda's lounge, he announced, "Linda, a confession: I have a daughter in Bucharest who was born in Romania after I ran away to escape family hostilities." It was blunt and a massive shock to her, delivered without empathy. Linda had many questions starting with the mother, the family and where and how they lived. Rather thoughtlessly, Jonathan added he was contemplating sending money to his daughter. The resulting debate was hard for him, as Linda became increasingly insistent on getting answers, and finally said in a raised voice, "What other great pearls of delight have you been hiding! And by the way, where are all your ill-gotten gains coming from?"

Not used to being challenged or, indeed, feeling anger from a close personal friend, Jonathan simply rubbed his fingers dramatically over his mouth closing his lips together. Then said "Maybe for another time" and walked out of the room. When the dust had settled, Linda was quick to notice a change, be it ever so small, in Jon's behaviour. Still attentive and polite but lovemaking was rougher, to the point of bruising and with some haste. Most times now lovemaking was just 'routine'. She tried not to notice but he blamed her for small daily errors, was picky about her food offerings, and very unusually for him, used language about things being 'fuck-ups'.

He tried sometimes to kiss and make up, but the subject was not in recovery and not much now made him happy. Jonathan was keen to defend the mantra he had used in his success. It was that to obtain status, reputation, and connections, you needed to be smart, clever, lucky and capable, and make big donations. It can take years, and all must be covered by a huge impenetrable umbrella.

Unbeknown to Jonathan his 'luck' was changing. The AFP now had an open active file on him, though not yet having a full database on all aspects of his activities. They knew he had well-disguised relationships with associates in the Crown Casino, gambling, money laundering, and therefore outlaw motorcycle gangs, but no known physical contacts with burglars or violence. A variety of connections were in operation to monitor his messages and communications. The nominated AFP officer was aware of Jonathan's 'innocent'? social contact with Superintendent Linda Alexander, and had been cautioned to be very careful.

Slowly bringing the situation to a head was the fact that the overseas crime syndicate was becoming much more aggressive, investigating what they considered the prospect of greater returns from their Australian turf. They were much stronger, and the relationship between them was changing; they now wanted to consider Jon as 'their man' and with that came expectations of much greater involvement and activity from him, particularly in relation to drugs.

Chapter 55

Australian Federal Police Background

The AFP investigates and prosecutes money laundering and serious financial crime that affects the Commonwealth or the ACT. These crimes are connected with serious and organised crime including the illegal drug trade, and crime syndicates such as the mafia. Crimes can include terrorism, espionage and foreign interference, drug crime, airport and aviation crime, crimes against children, cybercrime, serious organised crime, and fraud. The AFP Police Checks are the most comprehensive check available in Australia for an individual's criminal history. The AFP had shown interest in recruiting Linda into their ranks.

The AFP works with other Australian government bodies to investigate alleged criminal conduct, e.g. with the Australian Border Force. The Border Force performs Coast Guard and marine law enforcement duties and is a component of the Maritime Border Command, part of the National Intelligence Community and an active member of the World Customs Organisation.

ASIO—the Australian Security Intelligence Organisation—is the nation's security service. It collects, assesses and investigates intelligence or threats targeting Australian interests.

Whispers, flags, and rumours were arising in many quarters. The most likely scenario emerging was of an impending 'secret gathering' of organised crime in Victoria, which was going to host a range of invited 'likeminded interests' to consider further co-operation among the criminals. Quiet, low-level cooperation between these groups already existed. Known personnel invitees were from Fiji (a shipping expert), Indonesia, United Kingdom, Ireland, Vanuatu, USA and Columbia; some from cartels, and local Italian family members and bikie gang leaders.

The noose was tightening.

Chapter 56

Casino Conference

The date for the event was set under the guise of a 'gambling get-together' with all luxuries provided to known 'high rollers' of the world-wide gambling fraternity. They arrived from far and wide over several days, to be accommodated over various floors and suites at Melbourne's Crown Casino. Conference facilities were provided at different times and levels with strict security applied.

Many of the organised crime attendees were in fact also gamblers, so were supplied with generous quantities of chips to use as they chose. The get-together was primarily for selected international syndicate members, being a much more tightly controlled and exclusive group,.

Jon Smithson was invited to the exclusive protected gathering. Security was as tight as for any world leaders meeting imagined. He entered the premises through a back entrances, with some element of disguise. However, no matter how efficient and clever the disguise, extensive coverage by the national security services was in action. Listening devices, photographs, under-car devices and undercover personnel with differing targets everywhere, were tracking as many attendees as possible. However, no internal devices for recording meeting contents had been successfully planted.

Jon was sighted on occasions with contacts unknown to AFP or ASIO personnel. He did not gamble and rarely stayed out late. He caught cabs home and twice was accompanied in a private car by a distinguished-looking Irishman named Dermont MacDonagh—he liked his associates to call him, 'Sir Dermie'. At no time was Linda ever introduced to any of the attendees or to Jon's other cronies.

Beth contacted Linda and suggested a catchup in a cafe. They both ordered their usual half-strength long black coffee with cold milk on the side. After the usual 'hug and kiss' greetings, and checking that all was well with each other, they settled down and Beth looked around to be sure no one was eavesdropping.

Linda asked, "Beth, what's your problem?"

Beth replied, "Not really mine!" as she slid a large envelope across the table, and whispered "this is probably more than my job is worth!"

Linda immediately understood the importance of whatever was happening.

In a very low voice, Beth explained the photos had been taken in the past week or so by a paparazzi who regularly supplied some of his work back through an undercover police officer for favours. Beth went on to comment, as Linda viewed the photographs one by one, "These were taken on two different occasions around 11pm outside the Crown Casino front entrance, in spite of energetic efforts by security door guards to block photographing. As you know, organised crime is in town for a special event. The silver-haired man is known to UK police as an international crime syndicate leader from the UK; he's very big in drugs and he's a ruthless, vicious man, who likes to be called 'Sir Dermie'. Ancestral heritage there?"

Beth went on to state, "The other man getting into the chauffeur-driven car appears to be your Jonathan!"

Linda's face registered shock and horror, and in a shaken voice, she could only come out with a raspy, "Oh my God!"

Beth reached across for Linda's hands then stood up to reach across and hold her tight. Tears began to stream down Linda's face. Completely broken, Linda went further into a breakdown, sobbing, "What can I do?" realising the full horror of her position.

Beth and Linda left the coffee shop and walked quickly back to Linda's apartment to recover and discuss tactics. The full realisation of it all was only just beginning to sink in for Linda, when the morning edition of the 'Herald-Sun' newspaper arrived, featuring a similar photo on page 2 under the heading, 'Who is this man?'

A caption read: "Sources reveal the distinguished UK aristocrat at left, leaving a late-night crime syndicate meeting at the Casino, is Dermont MacDonagh (Sir Dermie to his friends), but who is the mystery Mr X beside him?"

Chapter 57

Repairs and Denials: The Inquisition

When Linda had recovered a little from the shock, she knew she had to put some space between her and Jon and the first thing to do at work was to seek a confidential senior level meeting for investigation, co-operation and guidance. She asked Beth to accompany her to the initial urgent discussion that needed to be held with her immediate superior, and the Personnel Manager.

Linda understood this would all probably be ultimately viewed under corporate governance policies and procedures, and legislation. To ward off any possible or probable complaints from the public arena she needed to act fast. A preliminary meeting was scheduled very quickly.

The inquisitive 'Herald-Sun' and other media went into action very quickly, and spent many hours digging for the Mr X. Armed with the photo and their contacts with paparazzi and underworld figures, talking locally to all and sundry, they were in short time able to come up with a name, as feared, a home location and occasional social contacts. It emerged that their named subject, Jon Smithson, lived in the same building as a senior police officer and in fact was in a relationship with her.

Linda's high-level police meeting began in a non-inquisitive manner with an officer taking notes. The title for Linda Alexander was Acting Superintendent to recognise her status. Senior Sergeant Jenkins was in attendance. The presiding officer indicated he was uninformed of details surrounding the agenda subject.

Linda volunteered a brief summary, and stressed the relationship was more than platonic but in no way contractual. They resided in the same apartment block but kept separate living conditions, security and privacy. They socialised together on occasion and were more than just casual friends. Linda advised she had introduced Jonathan to her parents but had little detail on his background. She had to admit that the background information he had given her was skimpy. "We enjoy time together, and I know he is an Australian citizen," she said. They did not have wedding plans in place. "We share no ownership of any articles such as property, furniture, cars, jewellery or cash," Linda stated. "We have no joint bank accounts."

That seemed to satisfy matters for the immediate discussion, and it was concluded by her superior that the matter would be referred higher up. No immediate suspension would be applied and at this stage no media release was needed. However the subject would be monitored daily and necessary steps introduced when appropriate. The senior officer thanked Linda and expressed appreciation for her swift action.

However, the rumour mill went quickly into action and enough people including police personnel were quick to speculate. Suggestions were whispered or offered to Linda and between others in lowered voices;

"I'm sorry, work from home for now and come back when you are ready."

"This must be one of the most difficult periods of your life, I know because I have been there!"

"Well, I suppose you know what they say, the average person files for divorce about two years after they get together!"

"I think the time apart will be good for them, wonder if they will find their way around and back together?"

"I wonder if he has contacted her. Men are trash. Every single man alive is a pile of actual trash."

"Maybe I could set her up with someone. My cousin is single. He's got a good job and is obsessed with Japan."

Linda knew that Jon must have seen the photo in the newspaper too, but he had not contacted her as yet. By accident several days later, Linda and Jonathan met in the foyer and almost by routine went to embrace each other, with Jonathan rubbing a familiar hand up her back, and they almost melted together.

Then she exploded, "You know Jon, I'm so sorry about this but I can't do it anymore!"

He looked sad as he nodded and moved on away from her.

In the meantime, in the background, inevitably, police progress was moving along very nicely.

Chapter 58

Sprung!

Jonathan Smithson

Tempus fugit (time flies). The old saying kept running through Jon's mind. He had often thought of the phrase as he had educated himself over many years and as his business empire had grown. He felt in a new and personal way now that time was running out for him to exercise certain options before the 'expiry date'.

Jonathan decided ask Linda for a few favours, ringing her and leaving a message: "Hi Linda, I can understand you do not wish to talk, and I apologise profusely for what I have omitted from my 'honest' confessions. Please forgive me. Can we meet for a quick very private talk in the coffee shop top of Collins Street opposite the tram stop? Private enough that we won't be seen, there's something I want to ask you."

Linda agreed, and they met. Linda was icy cold. Jon quickly stated his request, which was that a form of silence be observed. He went on, "I believe it's now likely that any communications between us will be monitored by ASIO and Australian Federal Police, and I know listening devices of many descriptions are already in place.

'Sir Dermie' is a big fish with many friends and enemies. Ordinary regular police will no doubt get into the mix. It's easy to suggest 'let's wait and see', but I believe the media followups will be vigorous and vindictive."

Linda's response was, "No, I am too hurt and wounded just for the moment, I prefer to leave it for a bit while I try to re-establish my equilibrium. I will contact you."

Jonathan returned home shattered, as he could feel his world crumbling around him. He poured himself, as his own crutch to bolster his strength, a strong gin and tonic and reflected on his situation; a wealthy middle-aged man with no friends or family. He was sometimes lonely but had planned and worked himself into that position as a matter of protection, and it suited him overall to be alone. He had to admit he considered Melbourne to be his home. He ran through in his mind the aspects of his contentment. The base of his luxury residence, the administrative centre for assets and control mechanisms. Alone in Melbourne, but securely so, he had always felt. Without a strong need to participate in community, and therefore no specific obligations, he could appreciate the attractions. A good-size diverse city, wonderful public transport, within three or four kilometres of his home seven theatres, a casino, multiple six-star international hotels, set amid 'all-season' parks and gardens, with a vibrancy created by new construction, university students and a constant flow of international sporting events using the MCG and other nearby stadiums that attracted people spending large amounts into the city.

From his home base, a rough circle existed to cover his most used and happiest parameters, from his Spring Sreet apartment to Flinders Lane then the Forum Theatre, St Pauls Cathedral, Federation Square, the Aquarium, Melbourne Ferry Terminal, Marvel sports stadium, Queen Victoria Market, Chinatown and the Greek precinct, all the theatres etc accessible on the City Loop by underground stations

Flagstaff, Melbourne Central, nearby Parliament station. Above ground, the beautiful and calming Fitzroy and Carlton gardens and the river walks to Docklands in the western end of town.

Jonathan wondered if his love for Linda was going to be his Achilles heel. He thought further on the reasons he was so contented in Melbourne. His apartment at the 'Paris end' of Collins Street was very close to upmarket retail shops, and the sirens from fire engines, police, and ambulances common to city life added to the colour. Overhead police and TV helicopters added to the mix but it all became just white noise after a while. The river with its Southbank developments, and its launches, cafes and stylish restaurants were within walking distance along Flinders Lane. While considering these virtues, he realised he also liked areas such as Lygon Street in Carlton, and Footscray, with their vibrant mix of residents and foods. And many other suburbs that he frequented less, or the Central Victorian towns like Castlemaine or Bendigo. He loved and regularly walked the intriguing lanes between Collins and Bourke Streets in the Melbourne CBD. It was exciting to attend jazz shows and music on the river. He was never bored! He had become, in fact, very Melbourne centre-centric. He had a strong appreciation of top-end restaurants such as Di Stasio Citta, right on his doorstep in Spring Street, which he could afford and frequented occasionally, but really preferred the simpler casual cafes and coffee shops.

With further self-reflection, he was aware he had no contact with anyone of Aboriginal background, and had no contact with large commercial companies or learning institutions. He really was a loner. Because of his wide international experience and travels he could to all intents and purposes hold intelligent conversations with almost anyone. The fact that he was wealthy enabled him to buy memberships in all sorts of clubs... He knew he was quite an enigma to others.

All these reflections got him closer to how he needed to respond to the genuine anger coming from Linda. And the realisation that he needed serious help to counter the media attention on him. He was racking his brains for how best to utilise his positive and understated qualities. Legal and high-profile recognisable community leaders were not his 'friends and relations'. In his prior life, he had regularly sorted out the best legal advice available and committed to them financial guarantees to seal in uncompromised advice to him. The first 'surprise' legal advice he received, which came from a big Melbourne firm, was to employ a certain Sydney legal group who had the reputation of being very 'flexible' and irregular. And expensive.

Jon mulled over what to do about Linda. Should he try again to involve her? Should he try just to meet again? And would she co-operate?

He decided he would try again. He was still confident of his position as he had not been contacted by any authorities, or the media, even though he was suspicious of this apparent quietness. However good or bad a situation is, it will change, he thought.

Chapter 59

Jonathan Requests a Meeting

Linda was seriously unco-operative but finally conceded to meet in a private meeting room at the RACV Club, with her best friend Beth Jenkins with her (no notes to be taken), and on the basis that it was to be no more than a casual meeting to discuss current parameters.

Agreed. As they had discussed they all turned up promptly, a little nervously, and Jonathan—who had never had a great sense of humour—tried to add some lightness by cracking a joke, "What does the Loch Ness Monster have in common with an intelligent sensitive Aussie? Some people believe they exist, but no one's actually seen either." As both were 'new Australians', it really didn't work that well but it got things moving.

Very tentatively Linda asked, "How ever can you repair the lies by omission you have spun me?"

With a certain amount of tiptoeing around the subject, Jon suggested that maybe the Chatham House rules—internationally recognised rules of meeting confidentiality—could generally apply to the discussion? Linda immediately responded, "Just remember Beth and I are police officers!"

Linda then went on the attack, "You requested this meeting, so please tell me, who are you really? What you do as work? What is your career? And who is 'Sir Dermie' aka Dermont MacDonagh?" She went on, "You know everything about me, from when I was a child, and yet I really know bugger all about you! That's so unfair!"

Hesitatingly, Jonathan responded, "I am a member of the 'Int IA'—International Inner Associates— a secret international society, and Dermont MacDonagh is the European leader.

"We are a small, exclusive group of men who affiliated into the group over years to achieve common goals. We best describe ourselves as 'fixers and arrangers'. We try not to break local laws, habits or cultures. That does not mean we have not done bad things to achieve our outcomes. We do arrange and facilitate buying and selling of some illegal merchandise — various products, such as drugs and chemicals, gold and diamonds, stamps, paintings, jewellery — with black market value anywhere in the world. We can eliminate things or people. We are traders, and there is a risk factor."

By virtue of his past actions and associates, Jonathan had become a sophisticated entrepreneur, he said to Linda and Beth.

On his current position, he felt he was in a trap and he had caught himself often dreaming of, or reminiscing on, one of his best remembered school poems, 'The Charge of the Light Brigade', a famous English poem by Alfred, Lord Tennyson written in 1854 on the Battle of Balaclava in the Crimean War.

Jon loved words from the first, best-known, stanza: "Half a league, half a league, half a league onward! Forward!" To his credit, he considered the third verse as being much closer to his actual current precarious position.

"Cannon to right of them,
Cannon to left of them,
Cannon in front of them
Volleyed and thundered;
Stormed at with shot and shell,

Boldly they rode and well,
Into the jaws of Death,
Into the mouth of Hell
Rode the six hundred."

It seemed very close to the position he had fallen into.

Linda strongly voiced her opinion, "That ignores the most important thing of all; integrity. What do you say about that, and what it all means? To us? Are you forgetting that all along you have known that I am a senior police officer who prides herself on her integrity!"

The reply from Jon was a simple, "Yes!"

Linda: "OK, then here are my simple questions, and the answers will decide whether there's any point in us speaking further."

Linda then gave herself some time to form a precis in her mind coveering her total feelings, then asked "I will need to know your full name and country of origin, and know all your family details, parents, and children. Any criminal records in Australia or abroad, and full details of your associations under any name!"

She waited while Jonathan appeared to give her questions consideration. While he hesitated, Linda added another request, "and while we are at it, I want to know how you have made your wealth."

Jonathan, being the good card player that he must be, looked seriously at Linda with great affection, totally ignoring the presence of Beth, and spoke, "With qualifications on all aspects of my responses, I can only respond, "No, to each request."

They then looked at each other in heartbroken resignation, stood up, nodded courteously to each other and prepared to leave.

Linda stopped, with one final request, "Please will you willingly supply to me material I need to establish a full ID?"

Going out the door Jonathan agreed: "OK." And then added,

"You know, I am clean; spotlessly clean, no drugs anywhere near me!"

Linda and Beth adjourned to their local pub, took over a corner and purchased two drinks; gin and tonic for both. Their low-voiced discussion was peppered with expressions of astonishment. Linda was shocked by Jon's revelations about his secret society. Hopefully the DNA material could be sent to US, European and southern African police counterparts for identification of Jon from the past? They also covered the new reality of the end of Linda and Jon's relationship and various ways progress could be made.

Linda was really rattled and needed the support Beth was providing. They agreed that the new information from Jonathan was to be referred immediately to Linda's superior for guidance, even though it could mean Linda's suspension. Her opinion now was that Jonathan had a large number of hidden associations that needed clarity. Sleepless nights for more than one, and intense use of the developing habit of contacting people at late night. What could be listened into?

Linda was of the opinion that her career, by association, was damaged, and she really missed her old father figure Ron Brunton within the force.

Beth encouraged her with an old chant they were both familiar with: "No matter how you feel, get up, dress up, and show up!"

Chapter 60

Beth Jenkins' Search on Jon

Beth was officially commissioned to begin investigations into who Jonathan Smithson actually was. Money, assets, friends, local, overseas, enemies... Where and when his name and passport were established, any outstanding legal affairs? Ownership of trusts, shareholdings, memberships? Any strange habits? The usual police digging and grinding away. Perhaps any DNA obtained from Jon may assist in his ID. Linda had recalled a snippet from Jon about his childhood in New York and his telling of being in Europe as a young man too.

Vic Police set up a major task unit with a direct connection to ASIO in Melbourne and coordinated correspondence with the United Kingdom, Europe and the US. It was a big taskforce. Beth was allocated staff to help with the routine research and authority to carry it out. Nothing was to be off limits.

The outline she gave to her team included investigations internally and external to Australia. Most of the offshore work had been designated to ASIO and a special contact was arranged between them. The FBI were also to be involved. Areas for special attention were legal debts and assets. The Malmsbury property ownership was to be investigated, and telephone records or other means of communications. Membership of clubs and organisations, and any shell companies to be investigated. Also rumours, disputes, accusations, secret memberships, politics—local or national activities, drugs for own use or trading. In this arena there were rumours of large-scale trafficking of methamphetamines.

Companions; he was known to have been with DI Alexander, but any other connections? Full details of all illegal contacts. Do not overlook any work done by private eyes in the past.

Motorcycles; it was known that Smithson owned a high-quality motorcycle that he had used on weekends, so grill any contacts with motorcycle gangs about possible 'respectable-looking' members. Even check with the law-abiding Ulysses Motorbike Club about their members aged around forty and over.

Beth's unit planned to 'tag' all future telephone calls between leaders and members of rogue gangs. Check on any friends, within or outside the police force, follow up any large donations made to anywhere! Get detail from trading banks. Check on use of couriers, chauffeur services.

Beth had a small team of four, and had been given a back office with all requisite facilities. Second in charge was a female sergeant who knew how to overrule procrastinations from above and how to motivate the two-single stripe constables. The four of them were like a boxful of fox terriers with energy galore and few constraints.

Their investigations emphasised how almost impenetrable the protection was that Jonathan had established around his persona. A significant part of the protective cover was his charm, politeness, likeability and reservation along with his wealth; that added to his mystery. The apartment block Concierge, George, prided himself on knowing everything going on in the building, but could offer little other than the arrival of a few items of mail from South Africa in the time that Jon had lived there, and he had held very occasional meetings in the lounge with an array of unidentified visitors, for no more than five minutes each. His international history was a closely guarded secret.

Beth was aware of an old saying that now applied to her as well to Linda, 'No one is in charge of your happiness, but you.' Information was not exactly flowing in and Beth naturally looked for help and direction from Linda, who of course had little or limited knowledge of personal details of his life in previous years.

Linda suggested to Beth that a call to her parents (John and Prue Alexander) in Perth may be valuable. Linda said she would ring them first to explain. Linda had taken Jonathan to Perth to meet her parents months ago and she recalled they had had lengthy late-night discussions about places in southern Africa. Perhaps some information more than Linda could recall from her memory of those nights might shine a light on directions the police could try.

Chapter 61

The Elusive Jonathan Smithson

Jonathan communicated to Linda by text with serious sadness, "I can't have you in my life any more."

It was apparent that he was well aware of the activity going on behind the scenes. A small story appeared in the Herald-Sun that Dermont MacDonagh was a major shareholder in a huge UK construction company used as a front through union members for his drug empire and people smuggling. Jonathan was admitting nothing to Linda or anyone else. He was going to ground, working on plans A or B as needed.

He knew he was vulnerable in two specific areas.

The first involved property holdings north-west of Melbourne in Caroline Springs, Taylors Lakes and Watergardens. Early on arriving in Melbourne, he had made some small anonymous property purchases. Tenants were unaware of Jonathan's background or identity, except they were occasionally asked for help or participation in some activity, which brought extraordinary rewards. These three or four tenants were invited for a chat about once a year at a nearby bowling alley to reinforce confidentiality.

Jonathan did change and disguise his looks over a number of years. He kept a moped scooter in a back garage from time to time but left it at Malmsbury more often, where he could go by train. Linda recalled he had used a Harley Davidson on at least two occasions for joy riding in the country.

His Watergardens cohort could be expanded without any personal involvement as needed. A casual morning cup of coffee with a group of elderly European men with discussions ranging over multiple subjects covered any nefarious associations that may exist. The group would break up, some men staying five minutes and some 45 minutes. No regular day or times set to meet, just random friendly meetings.

The second potential area of exposure involved Brunswick and Lygon Street, Carlton. For him, this was a highly dangerous area to operate both physically and financially. There were high stakes and high rewards, involving money laundering and gambling. His international crime connections had meant occasional contact but no close relationship. Really arm's length. Jonathan had had time to explore expos and conferences at will. He had joined and attended, all over Victoria, various groups and societies, usually with false details and under mild disguise if needed. A great base for loose information and contacts.

The constant digging of the police was certainly muddying the waters for Jonathan. As surreptitiously as possible, he began to tidy his affairs and pack up ready to make a seamless exit from Melbourne. In his usual subtle manner, he began to make enquiries about the Cooper Family Circus. Family situations, financials, and overseas connections. Investment needs or possibilities? Using his legal contacts to maintain anonymity, he established that the circus had moved with the times and was now very large, fully legally compliant and apparently successful. Owned and operated by the Cooper family, currently it was mother Cora and oldest son Marko who were in control. Circumstances decreed a very mobile and controlled set of assets.

Using a nondescript legal firm, he asked for an opportunity to meet them. Exhibiting no enthusiasm but a mild curiosity, Cora agreed that she and son Marko would attend a meeting in the legal company's offices.

There, Jonathan agreed to disclose his name and gave a succinct summary of his financial wealth and history back from arrival into Australia and his immigration from South Africa. He was a man of means. To try to create more interest, he falsely advised them that he had distant relatives in Scotland who had left him an inheritance; they were gypsies, their surname being Green. He added that he was aware that the Coopers could have gypsy heritage or connections.

Cora quickly denied any connections with any family called Green, and thought it sounded very British rather than 'gypsy'. Marko simply appeared mystified. The conversation was going nowhere but Cora suggested that Jonathan could leave his details in case some flicker of interest arose.

Jonathan was careful not to over-emphasise his interest but as a parting comment said, "My deceased uncle (Green) had suggested making grants to circuses as he loved them, but knew it was a tough and unique lifestyle." This could have been for reasons of nostalgia, he said.

After the meeting Jonathan thought all that had been achieved was a contact that may be useful in a future escape plan. No need to do anything further.

In the case of Cora and Marko, their conversation together was brief, "What the hell was that all about?"

Marko did not have a clue but it set off for Cora a long-forgotten memory of a specific family scandal and ructions she had heard about. A bounty had been involved... She would investigate.

Chapter 62

Jon's Plans

Jonathan was busy working on Plans A, B and C now, and potentially more, whilst Linda was working fulltime behind the scenes helping Beth and her team to establish real connections and identity. Every possible clue was followed. Jonathan became more aware of the pincers closing but even so he remained confident that his history was valid and hard to crack. As a nineteen-year-old fleeing his home country the US, he had been a swarthy young man with black hair and eyebrows, light facial hair, a trim figure, a US accent.

Now, he was forty years of age, greying hair, ginger-grey sculptured beard, a well maintained and polished look. He wore horn-rimmed glasses and evinced an occasional limp. He had a clipped, international-sounding accent, and held an Australian passport.

His major mistake was to approach Cora Cooper. It was just enough to raise a query in her mind that started some family reminiscing. Jonathan, in his defence, still felt confident in his attitude of; 'I'm no real criminal, I have no convictions, and I'm not guilty anywhere known!'

Linda was labouring emotionally at work, under the humiliation attached to her association with a suspected felon. It made her more determined to succeed in opening this Pandora's box and to prepare herself for life 'after Jonathan'.

Contacts of Jonathan's warned him of the police's detailed search and document inquisition behind his back and their apparent determination to flush out details. He began to carry large amounts of cash to avoid any tracking, and varied his daily disguises. His plans included the extensive use of cash resources that he had both in and outside of his apartment safe.

He had a Plan A: He had purchased tickets to fly to Los Angeles via New Zealand. Legal associates there were working on plans for him to assimilate into the underworld.

Plan B: A ticket to Dubai where he believed he could totally disappear and enjoy a lifestyle with criminal associates.

Plan C: He had a travel agent booking tickets to London and onwards into Europe.

Plan D: To disappear into 'remote Australia'. A circus hand? Motorbike connections?

Jonathan had become an extraordinary criminal, working in close association with international gangs and organised criminals. They operated outside groups such as the Calabrian Mafia, using the newest digital technology for cybercrime. They were truly professional teams, expert in encrypted apps and technologies and in the use of modern cryptocurrencies. Clearly, Jonathan was not competent in all this technology but he was associated with the gangs' strength and depth of criminal knowledge. Synthetic drugs were becoming bigger as were other fields of crime.

What he had overlooked was the new activity among the Codona tribe because of rumours filtering back about the bounty from the Cooper family in Australia.

The biggest mental asset he had was his grip on an old adage, "Keep calm under all circumstances!"

Little snippets of news appeared in the 'Herald Sun', on page 5 or 6, which did not allow the subject to totally die. A headline, 'Where is he now?' was followed by, 'We know where the infamous crook 'Sir Dermie' is — back in England! But where in Australia is our own Jonathan Smithson?' Adding helpfully, maybe at Crown Casino.

Such speculation added to the consternation of both Detective Beth Jenkins and DSI Linda Alexander. The most annoying thing of all was the unofficial question of whether Linda could indeed be a collaborator?

With or without wisdom, Jonathan decided to make contact with Linda. He sent a text using one of his burner phones. "Linda, my love, with huge apologies, let me confirm you had no part in collaborating with me knowingly or otherwise. I would like to meet for a chance to further explain." Friendly emoji attached.

Quick as a flash was the text response, "Not bloody likely!" The rule now 'Never the twain shall meet.'

Authorities were labouring away night and day and Linda was deeply involved. Beth and her team used all manner of media including profile photos released under the heading 'Person of interest.' Records were being searched and information accumulated even about small local airfields. Tthe acquisition of search warrants was being sought.

Naturally trying to avoid notice, Jonathan was busy calling in old favours and contacts. He hoped to quietly disappear 'down a drain pipe'.

Chapter 63

Demise of Jonathan Smithson

A late-evening call to the Melbourne Water Police told of the discovery of a body in Victoria Harbour adjacent to the Docklands Ferry Terminal. The body was a well-dressed male with a waterproof note on his chest saying "Enough is Enough!"

The ambulance crew were observant and commented that it looked like the deceased had been strangled before he entered the water; not a suicide. There were ligature marks and he had open, bloodshot eyes. His ankles were tied together.

Linda and Beth were among the first to be notified. They immediately recognised the deceased but would never know that the last words uttered by Jonathan Smithson were, "Who the hell are you?"

The killing of Jonathan Smithson complicated the existence of almost everyone who had been associated with him, though for some a huge liability had been removed.

Because he personally was not a notable or high-profile figure, despite the recent spasmodic press coverage, it was comparatively easy to keep media coverage low, but notice of the identity of the murder victim was sent to a large number of authorities.

Linda was devastated at this latest turn, despite the heartache that Jonathan had caused her with his deception, not to mention the potential professional damage. But with support from Beth, she said a sad farewell to this person who had so deeply touched her life.

It had not been easy losing Jonathan, but Linda now had to adjust to her new personal life, and, as she had always done in the past after a personal setback, dive with renewed energy into her police career. It helped that it now involved her new senior role as a Vic Pol Assistant Superintendent concentrating on police corruption.

The future lay before her.

After a long
commercial career
both overseas and
in Australia, Stuart
and his wife Jay have
lived 25 years in the
Macedon Ranges.